SKYRA *and* RIDALINE

Skyra *and* Ridaline

Katie Wilson

PARTRIDGE
A Penguin Random House Company

ISBN:	Softcover	978-1-4828-4646-1
	eBook	978-1-4828-4645-4

Print information available on the last page.

To order additional copies of this book, contact
Partridge India
000 800 10062 62
orders.india@partridgepublishing.com

www.partridgepublishing.com/india

Author's Note

Each chapter is titled either "FANTASY" or "REALITY", one after the other. "FANTASY" and "REALITY" are two different stories with Skyra, Ridaline and Bault as the common characters. Both these stories run in parallel. It can be said that "FANTASY" is in imagination, while "REALITY" is the real story.

PREFACE

Why do we meet the people we do in life? What decides that crossing of paths, that chance encounter with a person that can lead to intense upheaval of emotions, leaving the tale etched on our faces for the rest of our lives? Was it all already written when we were born that what people we might stumble across or...is it we who choose out of the plenty lot and decide what to do with them? Perhaps, there might be some invisible meshwork woven by every subconscious brain present in this world that creates pathways that make us form liaisons-sweet or dangerous, just like the dark matter which shapes the universe with the rare but disastrous result of two galaxies colliding with each other, sending reverberations all around.

The matrix out there, which I like to call the "mind pool" contains the chunk of mental piece contributed by each beggar, dictator, the waitress waiting at a table, the factory-owner, the bloke in the suit who rushes to the office everyday to fend off for the kids, the neighbour with the stuck-up nose. The pool is dense and vicious-and it works through the limitless links and connections-strengthened by words that emanate from the mind; and sometimes bound together by silence deeper than words could ever convey. The pool has murky traps hidden in it, waiting for the perfect prey to step into it at the first opportunity. The loose ends if not guarded, can lead to pitfalls........

Wars have been fought in history and whenever so, they have been noted down meticulously in books. There are many kinds of wars but a kind of which is never recorded are the psychological wars. The kind when the direct target is the "mind", not money or any materialistic needs or a pure joyous pleasure. A need that is seldom known-a mental hunger quenched by invasion on other's psyche- 'mind for mind's sake'.

How many of us have had a secret acknowledgement of understanding with a person, demanding no language; the unsaid being the strongest bond? A silent beating. A satisfaction guaranteed. People on different planes need words; rivals don't. A mental game with extension of all normal parameters of human tendencies, transcending beyond conventional boundaries. Sheer intolerance of somebody's being, distortion of all accepted laws- all reaching towards the summation of a clean victory.

CHAPTER 1

FANTASY

Skyra was the most beautiful woman of the country- nobody ever said that, but her sight reminded people of fresh lilies, of the silver lining in a cloud, of sunshine. She drew instant reactions, but was never unnoticed. Men gaped at her and women hated her for the same. She could feel comfortable in anyone's presence, while most people lost their ground in hers. Life lacked a certain spark for her, she often felt she was missing something in life but couldn't put a finger at it.

"Good morning, Your Highness 'The Queen of Prestoria'!! Would you like cheese or butter in breakfast?", said the maid, uncertain if she would get a reply from the bathroom.

The bathroom door clicked open and the blossoming beauty that emerged from behind wore a bathrobe wrapped delicately around her curvaceous body, drops of water trickling down the wet strands of hair.

The maid was in awe of her and Skyra knew that. She let some moments pass before she answered, "Mayonnaise", and began dressing up. The maid bowed and left. As she sat before the mirror, her gaze wandered through the window into the distant mountains. She suddenly opened the drawers, picked something up and deftly placed it on her palm- a donut-shaped metal bearing the insignia of Prestoria, underneath it the words emblazoned out in bold letters- "KING HAROLD-the 7th".

"Father...", she uttered lightly from the lips. 5 minutes later, she jolted back into reality and thought eagerly about the first screening of the play she was about to witness tonight at the theatre. Tripe, like all others-she mused. She hated the extra co-curricular duties that entailed with those of a queen. Nonetheless, as they say "whatever will be will be"-que sera sera.

But before that, she had another engagement that she had totally forgotten about. The Duke of Warrules would be shipping in this afternoon to meet her as a suitor. She had to hatch out some plan to get rid of him. Aunt Madeline has been acting out too much lately, what with this setting up. *Whoever is ready to get married?? I have hell of a lot to rule.*

Antonio Ragner arrived exactly at 2 o'clock as scheduled. But Skyra only came downstairs after an hour or so. The irked look on Aunt Madeline's face telling her what a trying time she had keeping the guest entertained. Partly, also due to the secret horror if she would ever show up or not.

Skyra didn't speak much, only pretended to listen which she was not quite sure of but decided she did a good job because Mr. Ragner blabbered incessantly about his worldly ventures and his passionate conquests for swords. Aunt prayed fervently that the meeting would go amicably and that the queen will behave. Skyra, on the other hand found herself mulling over the kind of women he went out with. *What difference does it make*, she spoke to herself, *if it's the Duke of Warrules of the Earl of Dreaton....? Just a couple of hours more.*

As soon as the trio finished their lunch, Skyra raised a toast and said, smiling, "May I have the courtesy of thanking dear Aunt Madeline for moving her magic wand and letting me know of your majesty's existence!!"

Aunt Madeline coughed up a bit. Then the queen abruptly rose up to her feet and announced, "I will meet you at 7 o'clock for the theatre. Don't say 'no'." Her sudden departure left a trail of breeze that left Ragner elated, yet dumbfounded. He waited eagerly for the occasion.

Skyra did not think about him until he saw his face in the evening. The people of Prestoria loved their queen. They greeted her with all the pomp and glory. She looked lovely and ravishing in the red gown, hair tucked up. Ragner might have as well passed off as her chauffeur!

"I have always said, Skyra...that you represent in beauty what your father did in bravery...", muttered Governor-general Sam Rodriguez.

"You are wrong. There is a beauty in bravery....", she said.

"Quoted out of context. But in an entirely different scenario, there is no immediate threat in saying that you are Prestoria's very own pumping heart...you make us feel alive..."

Skyra and Ragner sat in the centre box, the elite and affluent of Prestoria seated around them. In the middle as the play paused for a break and Ragner had gone to freshen up, her eyes laid upon a woman seated just across the aisle. She looked new to the place- just a minute little creature.

Their glances intercepted and Skyra smiled casually at the lightness of the moment. But the woman didn't reciprocate. Skyra suddenly felt an incompleteness of the moment. More than that, she thought that the woman did not belong here-in the same world as Skyra's.

Skyra continued to watch the rest of the play, commended the actors and director and Mr. Ragner was significantly mystified. He behaved strangely afterwards, as though something had changed in him. He knew the queen could never be his.

Prestoria did not have any complicated history as do many lands; no dark past. It was a peaceful country which boasted of gallant kings and gay citizens. The blissful atmosphere was all its men knew of. Vibrant and pristine. Shepherds liked their sheep and women loved their orchards. The country was governed under strict law and order which generations of fine rule had established. People wore the badge of being a Prestorian like a medal of honour. It was a land which Skyra loved and if there was any country she had to be associated with, it would be Prestoria. "*I would never trade my role in this world with any other, that's how lucky I am*", she used to tell herself.

"You are one in a million", her father would say. Before he died of yellow fever. "Keep the spirit alive", were the last words he said before he bid farewell. At 21, Skyra saw the crowd waving to her as she reclined on the throne. The princess had become queen. The ministers spoofed on their ruler being so immature, let alone the fact of her being a woman. "Women!! They got their brains in their knees.... Just enjoy the show as she walks into a pickle...."

Needless to say, there were several conspiracies brewing during the time of the king's death, including poisoning the princess with atropine. But Aunt Madeline's strict vigilance kept such possibilities at bay. Lecherous ministers desperately wanted Prestoria to fall under financial crisis so they could plough in at the right time. But nothing of that sort happened. If anything, Prestoria's economy only got better-reaching the highest pinnacle ever.

Skyra proved to be a dexterous ruler. She would listen to troubles and problematic situations for hours at a time and speak little at the end, asking the speaker to pause when she had to process information. After some initial glitches she made in the beginning, she learnt and never goofed up again. The more she learnt to follow her own mind, the fewer mistakes she made. No official could commit the crime of reporting late. They did not have the freedom to like or hate her-they just had to accept her the way she was. Some men could not get accustomed to the idea of being ordered around by a lady; but somehow they learnt to bend their knee. Nobody questioned or disrespected her anymore. She was hailed as the "enigmatic empress".

Nobody knew where the weaknesses of their queen lay. She seemed impervious to the most hostile person present. They concluded that it would take a person of the fourth dimension to really affect her and that the kind of person didn't exist either.

"Do you know for instance, my dear, what happens when it accidently slips from a farmer's mind to spray his grapes with insecticide...??", said the Aunt, offering Skyra the glass of fresh orange juice kept on the table.

Without waiting for an answer, she said, "The bacteria finds its way into it and corrodes it from inside. The grapes can't be eaten then...They lose their worth…Ultimately, the tree becomes useless...", she looked at her straight into the eye.

"I'll keep that in mind if and when I do plan to produce wine", said Skyra smugly.

"What I mean is my dear, look at you! You are so young and naive!! You have no idea what colour the world shows you...What you see when everything's picture perfect is just mirage! Keep a leash on yourself...Otherwise you might make enemies and the next thing you know, the bacteria has had a field day...I'm saying this as a protector-guardian because now that Harold is not here anymore, it's my duty to take care of you...Don't look at me like that... And for heaven's sake, get married!! You don't want to live your whole life doing a man's job, depriving yourself of all womanly rights..."

"Yes I do...!!! And speaking of that, what a teabag Antonio Ragner was...!! I didn't do much justice to him... you should've seen his face....", and she burst out laughing.

"Now, if you don't agree to change your attitude....."

CHAPTER 2

REALITY

When the girl woke up, she remembered nothing else of the dream so vividly other than the woman she had met in the theatre. That emotion lingered, every other feeling had evaporated. It was a strange heaviness, like some sharp wedge had penetrated into the innermost recesses of the brain and created a realm of its own. It was not disturbing, to say the least, but what was actually disturbing was that why did it have to be important enough to leave such a strong mark? She had seen Mrs.Krummer once or twice from the balcony. It had not been even a month since the Krummers had moved into the next door of her apartment building. They were a curious couple. Preferred to remain in their own module, had some lines drawn or so. The wife was not extremely attractive neither the husband any better, but both appeared to bask in their own standard mostly maintained by keeping a high-strung demeanour. Their aloofness seemed to be more than a necessity, like a safety weapon that had to be present at all times lest someone pop their bubble and expose them to the repulsive exterior. To make matters worse, every time Skyra had had an encounter with them, the guards had gone upper.

What the hell, she said as she crept out of bed and remembered that she had to report at her Fashion House at 9:30. On her way in the streets, she passed a lingerie store called 'Queen's Den' and was suddenly hurled back into the dream she had had this morning and thought curiously if there were actually a parallel universe out there where there was a country called Prestoria and she were actually playing the multiple role of a queen. An alter ego. She slapped her head and chided herself.

Fransisco Quinto, the owner of Ballerina Fashion House, considered her the 'crème de la crème' of the organisation.

"Look at her walk", he would say to the other models, "The sway, the lift of the head, the oomph and yes....the panache...I want to see that in each one of you. If you don't have it, fake it..!!!"

"Élan is coming up with a title of "Fashion Futurista" of the year. Who do you think it's gonna be...??", said Sophie, her tresses wound up in curls backstage.

"Are they...?", said Skyra, biting off an apple.

"Be ready girl, to hog the limelight. Pride and glory. Give them all bitches yet another reason to swear and fume...."

"That's weird. I didn't think you liked me much," said Skyra.

"It's a matter of size and distance".

Few days later after a major show, in the dressing room, Sophie asked, "Wanna come over for a bite? They got great sandwiches just around the corner."

At the restaurant, Skyra said all of a sudden, "Someone hates me."

"Everybody hates everybody these days. It's weird you give a shit."

"No, I don't...But it's a little different than that- might be loathing. Like some guilt thrust upon you regardless of some crime you may or may not have committed. Have never witnessed this degree of alienatic behaviour in life- on myself."

"Who are you talking about?"

"A woman next door. Practically a stranger."

"Might be jealous. Or a little bit insecure."

"There is even some privilege in jealousy. But she makes me feel like...like an unwanted garbage bag...like a stigma".

"Relax and gobble down your sandwich. You might be painting a much worse picture...You're not one to let someone get into your skin..."

"I keep getting this inkling of some impending danger I have to brace myself against...I don't know what it is, but it is like a silent threat. Whenever I look at her, I see a storm brewing", she was staring at a distant point, a neon bulb gleaming over the counter.

"Oh, what nonsense are we talking about...? Tell me, what do you think of Fransisco's latest spring-summer collection? The colours are bland, if you ask me...and those frills!!! Oh my God, the frills!! They looked so crass...!!"

But Skyra wasn't listening. The words that came out were faintly audible under her breath, "I can't nullify my existence, can I...??"

In the 3 months that followed, Skyra had formed a tacit understanding with her neighbour and her husband-bitter in taste. Only the unspeakable was the bond of connection between them-the language of the unsaid having the strongest impact. Whenever possible, she tried to steer clear of them, openly avoiding them because sight of them left an unexplained and uneasy pit in her stomach, a sense of deterioration. On the other hand, when she went into the balcony, she often found the woman, as if waiting and knowing that she would come. Then Skyra would again feel that pang of sinking feeling, deeper than the last she had. Skyra had outgrown the shock of such unexpected meetings but at the end of it, a question mark always seemed to pose itself every now and then.

It did not take her more time to realise that her neighbour was playing with her mentally. But it all looked to be a neat and friendly game from outside. The woman looked at her as one would look at a dangerous weapon which also possessed the brilliant dazzle of a diamond. It seemed to appear that she wanted something from her-perhaps the shiny part. She always observed Skyra with unflinching attention, weighing her heavily as if Skyra held a value attached to her own personal wealth. She always seeked to look at Skyra directly into the eye, trying to gain entry into an uncharted territory. Such interactions were the only means of communication between them and they rendered a bridge of closeness, which Skyra was not too glad to have. She often felt the presence of some unknown force encroaching on her mental premises.

One curious aspect of the couple was the relationship between the wife and the husband-the husband was a worshipper, a true devotee of his wife's persona. A vanguard for her and proud enough to declare it. An invisible spring was wired to his brain, so that whenever he was away from his house, he would find the way back safely and get relieved of the pressure upon reaching the headquarters. He looked like a kid whose mother has made him memorise his lessons in advance of the teacher's class. *Has him by the neck*, Skyra thought to herself.

Lately, the wary attitude of the man towards Skyra had escalated, combined with a heightened sense of superiority. Men did not behave normally like this, there was an air-pump inflating his vanity. He appeared to look like a person on a mission, brimming with confident energy, who knows where he is going and what he is doing, that nothing could injure him and anyone who dared to cut him in his path will be diminished to the ground. A tumultuous current was building up, it was evident and the husband was neck-deep in it. Skyra knew where the core of the current came from and felt a throb of undesirable resentment taking space in her.

Skyra noticed a changing pattern in the woman- her gradual metamorphosis into a lady exhibiting intellect and finesse. She looked more composed than ever and confident with her looks. Skyra was as indifferent to the new avatar as to the dust below her shoe-wedges, but it seemed the woman really wanted it to affect her and desperately searched for some hint of jealousy in her face whenever she passed her.

These days Skyra had even been hearing her voice more frequently. Ridaline usually talked in a screeching voice, slicing all other overtones across, not letting any point survive. Afterwards, she would emerge as an entirely different person, like a refined young woman and would look at Skyra with gleaming malicious eyes. Once, Skyra overheard what appeared to be an argument between the couple-the woman spewing venom like a serpent, the husband cleanly beaten. A dominating Xanthippe. What is she taking reins of, she thought. A part of Skyra's heart went out to for the poor husband, but perhaps the husband preferred it-being led.

"The secret behind a great runway success is the make-up", quoted Timm Valance as he brushed the cheeks of Betty Crow. "Without proper touch-up here and the correct stroke there, models would look as mere humans, not as the exquisite plastic mannequins churned out of a factory."

"There are exceptions, of course. Like there is one in your group, who I would not like to name and I'm sure we all know, who encompasses all the charisma it takes to set the ramp on fire. Make-up and the dress appear trivial on that luscious body. A real sex goddess descending from the heavens. Of course I don't mean to demean you....But there is a Queen bee and then there are worker bees....."

"Every dog has it's day….."

"When will yours come...?"

"Soon. Careful Timm, I think your strokes are going awry", said Betty when he paused to dabble the brush on the palette.

"Are they...? My bad...You are a charm sweetie, what would I do without you?"

"I'm getting a fancy on you. When you're done with your strokes, consider giving me a chance to stroke your......"

The piece Skyra wore was a knee-length dress with intricate artwork on a green background.

It looked elegant and genteel on her tall and thin frame. It reminded any on-looker of a pristine mountainside and yet the ferocious appeal of a pop star. The outfit's horizon and vitality seemed to be exalted beyond the admiration it deserved. The dress would not appear so intensifying on any other model.

Skyra did not have to choose the costumes, the costume chose her. Anything she wore, looked like it belonged to her, like a part of the body she carried. Her demeanour and style would transform accordingly, finding the perfect rhythm, almost resonating with every thread of the fabric. The lines of her hands, legs and neck aligned with that of the garment, as if it were caressing her body.

"The fitting's loose here", she said, referring to the neckline of the the dress.

"We don't need any last-minute glitches. Improvise. Here we go", said the assistant, tucking her dress with a pin.

"It's not your fault honey, but you will still make heads turn," and he showed a thumbs-up sign.

When she strutted across the stage, she did not see the sea of anticipatory faces before her eyes. They seemed to vanish underneath her line of vision into some faraway spatial configuration; her body tightened with an upcoming surge of energy and emitted a flamboyance unsurpassed. It was a race car, she seemed to be possessed by a harmless devil. It was exhilarating for her, she didn't know about the others.

"You owned it", said Sophie afterwards as they boarded the bus together, "Betty looked sore."

When Skyra got down at her stop, she let her hair down and let in a fresh breath of air into her stifled lungs.

The glamour, the artificiality had got in too deep inside; the competitiveness of unworthy opponents that acted as stumbling blocks, evading it; expelling it all from her mind, ironing out the imprints left by innumerable people she saw and never remembered later; she let it all filter down to only one feeling – that it was her life and the joy she experienced in it could not be replaced by anything else. She gazed up at the sky, the stars splattered like glinting candle-dots and wished the sky would swallow her into its magnanimity.

They arose into the picture like a click of switching on lights in a dark room; and a sufficient time elapsed before Skyra's senses became fully aware of the presence of the approaching people. The silence was pin-drop. It was like a meeting of strangers too familiar with each other. Skyra felt the sharp poke of a dreadful coldness gripping the atmosphere. Never before in her life had she been acquainted with the seriousness this kind as she ascended the stairs with her neighbours.

In the mutual silence that accompanied, she walked to her apartment door, but before she could jiggle her key into the keyhole, the sound of slamming of the door behind her knocked the wits out of her.

She entered into her apartment room and switched on the lights. Her fingers moved automatically; she was not making any conscious effort, but like a duty she was ordained to perform. She could not take in the moment of halt, she had to do something. The refrigerator loomed in front, she promptly went towards it and extricated a can of orange juice. Like a person still caught in the pandemonium of the preceding moment, she poured the juice into her mouth. She was not aware of how the liquid felt like, only that the events were happening correctly. She did not know what to do next; but the urge to take action was gigantic and immediate. Exasperated, she lied listlessly on the sofa and let the emptiness confront herself. The stupor lasted for 17 minutes.

When she finally got a grip on herself, she dragged herself to change; the show today seemed like some distant memory of a past life. The shock she had been pushing aside now came to surface, it seemed to bear down on everything around her-the TV, the curtains, utensils, even the dinner she had. When it finally occurred to her that she can't concentrate on anything else anymore, she slumped down on her couch like an immovable wounded bird. Her mind was trapped in a maze and it would be forever if she didn't let herself cry. That was the only way to re-establish her connection with the ongoing reality. It felt not exactly like death albeit like a close one-a psychological murder.

Chapter 3

FANTASY

The sky had darkened, the clouds roared to announce the approach of a thunderstorm. People of Prestoria lay inside their homes, snuggled together to absorb the warmth of the fireplace. The cattle bellowed while the wolves shrieked into the beaming luminosity of the scarred moon. The windy air swept the stiff leaves into its momentum, picking up grains of dust in its wake. Amidst blinding lightning, Skyra stepped out of the palace, overlooking the bewildered expressions of the guards. She ventured into the forest, defying the warning of the upcoming squall. She knew something had terribly and drastically gone haywire. She had to find the answer. She was aware of the precariousness the weather brought with it, but she desperately wanted the overture to show itself. She had barely reached the banks of the river when the downpour started. Stopping in her tracks, she took shelter under a tree. But her heart was still thumping forcefully.

"Brushing with danger is not for innocent kids. Didn't your mother teach you to always stay within the safe limits?"

Skyra twisted her head to the left to behold the female standing behind her. They stared at each other. Skyra tried to recall where she had seen the face before. Her eyes fluttered instantly when she finally recognised her. The theatre.

"How did you like the surprise? Did it hurt much, what I did to your Utopia? The turning of tables......"

Skyra listened.

"That's a rhetorical question, I suppose. And oh, how inhumane of me to ask- adding insult to injury...A sophisticated dainty girl like you belongs inside the walls of a palace..."

There was a momentary pause, as if the woman waited for Skyra to respond. But it didn't come.

"You would never possess the cunning it takes to match wits with me. On second thoughts, your respectful attitude won't allow either....The so-called 'conscience'...."

"What do you want...?", Skyra was tempted to ask.

"I can't ever embody the exuberance you radiate- and that is your biggest ornament and your worst crime. You will give that to me now. You are too pure to get jealous, I tried and failed. But I am thoroughly informed of your weakness- your virtue, your principles, your ideals.....A flower like you will be crushed, and every time I succeed, the world will be coloured in my hue, more and more...With every satisfaction I get from trampling you, I will get stronger and superior...I will change the face of this earth forever....I must thank you for being there to inspire me into such a dream.... Your struggle to escape destruction is my ecstasy and it will provide me the path to fulfil my vision...I am dependent on you, you are my guide from today, In fact from the day we first met....."

She continued, "The innocent are sacrificed to pave way for the master-minds. Tell me, does any way exist till I manoeuvre you into a well-layered mental cage, until you give up trying to break free...?"

"Whether you keep mum, or struggle to cross swords with me, the odds are in my favour. This is a new beginning. Your hunky-dory phase in now over and your merry-making Prestoria is now going to be slain into the history books by me. In place of it will rise a country ruled by me, people burning their blood and sweat to worship me. And you will have no other option than to let them...When I have that beautiful sight in front of me, I shall have had my victory......"

The storm was beginning to set in. The drops that replaced the drizzle now were huge and pounding heavily on the trees. Hails kept falling every now and then.

"Meet your enemy, Ridaline....", she extended her hand but Skyra stood, hypnotised.

It was only when she vanished that Skyra discovered she was drenched with water. Absently, she thought about returning back to the palace. Aunt Madeline would be mad.

But she realised she could not find her way back to the Bloomburg Palace. There were trails everywhere, but they did not lead anywhere. There were paths, but no destination. She looked around, helplessly searching for an end. The storm had broken in full raging fury. She fainted.

Chapter 4

REALITY

Waking up to the sun-kissed morning, Skyra opened her eyes to face the ceiling. Her head felt heavy as if she had a hangover. The event of last night flooded back. Last night had been the most incredulous night of her life-ethics had been broken, boundaries had been transcended. She felt that all that she was, her achievements, her self-esteem had been furiously attacked and transferred to make the jewel for someone else's phony crown, swell up the riches of someone else's fortune. She felt herself being pushed unwillingly to make space for the flourishing of a demon. She was aware of only one thing-that she had a conscious enemy lurking around. It had been a wake-up call.

A part of her brain which she had never previously used had been ignited on. She was aware of two things-that the woman hated her personally and secondly, that Skyra was incorporated in her subconscious. She had had a first touch of what she accepted as evil. This is what anti-matter must have been like, the nemesis of matter, in the beginning of the universe. The field difference was great and the flux of vanity was colossal. She had been made to understand what words could never say. Only one reason could explain this- there was a vying for a common coveted position in the hierarchy. She thought curiously that the silence between them was taken for granted by her, it concealed the actual equation. The woman hated her repulsively, but she had now let it known to her purposely; this fact itself reflected how strong she considered herself and how determined she was for the future. It was like an open invitation to challenge. But by openly expressing her real motive, she had also unknowingly dropped an important clue to her own weakness-that Skyra irked her.

Skyra realised that the invader had trespassed into her brain and now she had to build a wall that would not permeate further advancement. She had to check her vulnerability. The most horrifying fact that presented itself was that her brain had been getting mapped since long; when she could not care less, a person nearby was contemplating days and days out and nights on end to probe into her mind. The present explained the theory behind the past. Skyra's ignorance had done her in, but how was she supposed to know? She had never faced an adversary this kind. It was already late. She knew that the woman lived in a world of her own which was hinged at some fixation point. But hardly had she known that Skyra herself was at the centre of its gravity. Someone likes to feed on mind, a relish that even money can't buy. She decided to muster up her energy and bring out the fighter in her.

The only way she could proceed was by being exactly what her enemies wanted her to be- the targeted helpless victim. No, there is not the highest dignity in that, she knew. But she won't retaliate, she won't let them know of her own animosity- it would be like deliberately converging her life with hers. Or coming down her pinnacle by granting Mrs. Krummer the brand of enemy. Placing her in the same spectrum as her own- a honour that she will take down well-in other words, an utterly wrong move.

She would put the ball in her court. First, she had to observe the extent she would chart one-sidedly, only then Skyra could act or decide. Skyra would put a psychological net on them. They were experimenting with her-she would carry out her own experiment on them. Never in any age, or by any means would she accept her dominion. Nobody can mould me their way, she affirmed. Let's play along.

"When things aren't going your way-remember the ABC rule. Adjust, bow or cave in...", said John Pinter, son of Alfred Pinter, her father's friend, when she was in 1st grade. "This is what my grandpa told me...."

"Yeah...? What about fighting....??", she countered.

At 17, sick and fed up of the dreariness of her parents' unhappy and decaying marriage, she had ran away from home; from Marseille to Paris to a friend, Patricio she had met in a summer camp. She had stashed a bundle of hundred-euro bills that her mother kept in the closet into her pockets and slinked without any prior notice. She knew nobody would care to look for her because they were expecting something of this sort to happen. Her father, a confectioner would spend most of his day at the drinking bars, while her mother would spend her hours with the newspaper-boy, undisturbed. Now that she was on her own, nostalgia would drive her to call home every once in a while.

Patricio had found accommodation for her to stay as a paying guest in a decent locality, while she worked part-time in a restaurant as a waitress, then as a typewriter at a solicitor's office among other things. She also enrolled herself in a university. Until one day, when he slid his hands inside her jeans and offered to teach her things. She never saw him again. Men always kept an eye out for her; she would smile and respond back charmingly, but she had not been drawn to anyone in any serious manner. Lonely evenings found her wondering at times, if she would ever have a shot at a romantic life.

It was at the Great Meridian at Willington Street, where she had taken up job of as a receptionist to kill summer vacation when the director of a local magazine, when asking for the keys put her a proposal to work in a shampoo advertisement. She agreed and found work after another. She had soon started to give other top models a run for their money. When she got chosen into Ballerina, she was already known in dynamic fashion circles as "the suave pin-up". Time had taken its own course and floated her into its turbulence, upstream. Life had been exciting, to say the least. She had grown a penchant towards the runway, the dresses, the galleries of the fashion world. She had even been featured on the cover page of 'Sultry Town', 'Passion Stop' and 'Fascination'. Designers digged her. But a particular group that especially disliked her also existed. A well-known magazine went as far as to term her as "controversial". She always evoked extreme reactions from the mass. Not many could delve into inside her "high-headed" attitude and become a friend, but those few who did found an exposed and extremely soft centre, almost childish in nature lying inside the tough coat of indifference. They found her uncomplicated, yet mesmerising. Women longed to impersonate her, but were astounded by her too.

"Will you water my flowers, darling?", Riddy said plainly.

"You mean now....?", Bault said, engrossed in the business magazine he had been trying to decipher, which a friend had suggested for a good and informative read.

"You wouldn't....?", she said, looking deflated and empty.

"I will go right up", he said, losing all interest in the magazine.

Finishing his duty, he came inside, eager to get back to the business article he had been carefully scouring. The top-notch feel he got from the prospect of discussing the high-tech article with colleagues at office was unmatched. It would certainly make him stand out from the boring and drawling lot and raise his standard in front of others. Put him in an entirely different league.

No sooner had he stepped inside, than he found his mouth stuffed with sweet creamy taste.

"I made it....for my baby....", said the wife, smiling.

The pineapple cream pie exploded inside his mouth, and infused him with a pleasant happiness for his wife and the world in general. He felt blessed to be alive and to be in the world where he exactly was. He felt like a happy and satisfied man, a reward which he deserved and which could not be stalled any further. This is what real bliss feels, what the sages tried to discover centuries ago-he thought, soaking in the ease and the mildness of the moment. He had never before felt so comfortable at home and in the arms of a caring wife, he was proud. Riddy was changing and he appreciated it. She seemed at peace and happy with her home-bound duties. He liked when she was being extra sweet-it was becoming to her. He wondered why he had never seen her in that element before- not even during their short courtship. He liked especially when she took special care of his breakfast, lunch and dinner-it had her love showered on it.

"We are expecting the Fergusons tonight for dinner", she said, rising from the sofa. "You realise we do need to socialize, don't you...?? I am even opening the new crockery for them. How did you like the pies…?"

"The best thing about a get-together like this is the loosening-up. We all need an outlet to release our strain and be friendly with each other. Or else what would be left of life...??", said Fred Ferguson, lounging on the sofa. The dinner had been scrumptious, consisting of chicken and fried rice followed by sorbet.

"Exactly", asserted Bault, echoing his synchronous thought. "It helps us relax...you know, forget the world for a while…"

The four of them engaged in a chit-chatter.

"Frankly, the chicken was out-of-the world. Where did you learn to cook chicken in wine...??", said Emily Ferguson.

"I will give you a copy of the recipe if you like. It must be lying somewhere. Though, I am not sure it will turn out the same way...", said Riddy, "Don't worry, it will."

"This is one ashtray. Where did you get it from...??", asked Emily, looking at the ashtray inside the glass cabinet.

"You like it...?"

"It's unique. Looks expensive. Last time I saw one at the flea market, they said 50 euros...I just stared open-mouthed.. like 'Are you kidding me?'"

"This one belonged to a vintage shop in Monmarte Avenue. To the likes of Elizabeth or the Tudors, either one, I don't remember exactly who. Seriously, what kind of a cheap taste do you reckon I have...?", cooed Riddy.

It was not meant to be offensive, Emily wondered why she felt precisely the same for a fleeting second. She did have a bad taste, afterall.

Abruptly, Ridaline rose up and promptly went inside. She carried a solid thing in her hand, which was about 3 feet tall in size, covered with a white cloth. She set it cautiously on the table. Then she clapped her hand and announced, "I am using this occasion to unveil my latest sculpture I have been busy carving this week. Took a bit longer than I planned but eventually, it did come out the way I wanted it to."

"Surprise!!! I hope you like it", she chirped and removed the cloth with a swagger to reveal the thing it hid beneath.

The piece was ivory white. It appeared to be a crane, standing with one leg flexed and holding a fish inside its sharp extended beak. She smiled as she saw it- her eyes fixed to it, unblinking.

CHAPTER 5

FANTASY

Skyra was jerked into wakefulness by the sunray piercing on her eyelids. The distant sound of a peacock came intermittently. She sneezed as she lifted herself up from the ground. The ground was moist and her gown too. The events of the last night flooded back to her.

She saw an old haggard man, carrying a heavy bag on his back that made him stoop a little, passing by. He wore tattered shoes that made a peculiar sound as he trudged his feet.

"Hello", she called out.

The old man stopped to look at her. He examined her with curiosity and surprise, the most empathising eyes Skyra had ever seen. Just as she he was expecting to be recognized, he turned and went on.

Skyra rushed to his side and said urgently, "Excuse me, I seem to have been lost and can't find my way. Would you be so kind as to guide me to Hauris Point?" She thought it better to hide the fact of her royalty. The old man must be new or senile.

"There is no Hauris Point over here. The city is 2 miles from the forest."

She stared, nonplussed. "But this isn't Prestoria...?"

"You on drugs...?"

She quickly explained: "Oh, I am awful in reading maps. Actually I came with a couple of friends for some hunting and adventure. But the storm..."

"Yeah the storm was quite fierce last night. Haven't seen any like that in entire lifetime in Helfung. What a bad day to choose for fun!"

"I need to go back to Prestoria.."

She gazed around to find some other person in sight, but the stretch was empty as far as she could see. Someone else could help her better, might even identify her and pay their respects as people usually did. How she ever wandered into this part of Prestoria would forever remain a mystery.

But the more she walked on, more the place seemed unfamiliar. As the wilderness cleared, they halted near a pick-up carriage. Panting, the man put the bag down with a thump. His carriage was full of similar bags, five or six in number. Skyra peeked inside one of them. Apples, they contained.

"This is ma oldie wagon", he said, patting it from the side. "Now, if ya want to go to the city, hop in lady. That's all I can do for ya. John didn't come, he's sick with fever...or you would have had to climb into the oldie's back..."

Skyra dimly thought that as a Queen, she was probably having her most unhygienic ride. This would be a story to pass on. She got inside, but grimaced as the worn and torn seat started poking her behind. The engine whirred and the carriage started moving.

"What a bright day! Unbelievable... After the night-long raging battle, finally there's peace to greet....", he commented as they sped along the street, knocked-out trees on the way retelling their story. Suddenly, he said in a grave manner, "Any idea where your buddies might be....?"

The truth had not yet sunk in. But it stayed, suppress as she may. When she alighted the carriage, she squared off with the town. This was not her land. Nobody knew her. As she slowly tried to come to grips with this undeniable and unmistakable fact, she thought of the woman she had bumped into last night. She had taken it from her. Her Prestoria was stolen. And she was trapped in this illusionary world that stood in its place now..........

"*I have to find a way back...I have to find a way back...*", Skyra kept repeating to herself. She felt herself stuck in some abysmal pit. Moreover, she didn't quite like this place; it was like anything but Prestoria. There were people blabbering like programmed robots. To top it all, there seemed to be no individual space; it reeked of inferiority as its anthem. It was getting overbearing for her.

She found herself badly missing her homeland.

She strolled quite a considerable distance, observing people and cursing her condition, till people started to appear more frequently. A group of thugs were sitting outside a wine-shop; they whistled and bared their teeth lecherously. She was beginning to feel sick and dirty... and an indispensable burden to stay dull and inferior kept looming before her. She approached the busy city centre. It had an extended colosseum-like arena, with a string of pillars intercepting from 2 sides. There were posters glued to the walls. Skyra squinted to look closely- it had the picture of Ridaline with the words printed underneath it- "The Countess has arrived!!!"

A cold feeling enveloped her. She confronted the nearest person in sight, a merchant-shop owner and asked him, "Excuse me...The Countess...Do you know where can I meet her? I am new over here", she said it, the imposed calmness betraying the anxiety in her voice.

The man eyed her suspiciously. He won't reply.

Skyra obediently left and spotted a fruit-seller, and went up to the lady. She made a longer-than-usual eye-contact with the fat bosom lady, then said, holding a fruit in her hand without interest,"Nice mangoes...Are they fresh?"

The lady made a petulant face and placed the mango back into her cart. "Won't sell if they weren't...", she replied.

Then Skyra extended her hand and tactfully flashed the sapphire ring lodged in her index finger.

The lady sighed and leant back.

"The Countess", said Skyra flatly.

"I would like the reward first...", said the lady.

Skyra loosened the ring from her finger and placed it on the lady's palm, without pulling her hand away.

"Violet Valley, straight from left...", the lady spat. She could not imagine what reason could have lead the girl to trade such a precious stone for the useless information. She stared at the ring and smiled in glee at her first lucky earning that day.

Violet Valley was about half a mile east from the town. Skyra reached it on foot. A huge castle rose before her eyes. It was guarded by several uniformed men who patrolled around it.

Then, she heard noises of clinking and of men. Swirling around, she perceived a structure looming up in the distance.

Several workers were engaged in lugging heavy stones, setting them in place, one over the other. Incompletely-built pillars, shafts and beams lay hither and thither. It looked like initial workings for the construction of an edifice set in a vast expanse. As she began to wonder what it was, she met a large square-cut stone embedded in earth. It read:

"The Inescapable Prison"

CHAPTER 6

REALITY

The effects of what transpired the previous day could not be any more unmistakable than what unfolded there on. Skyra was astonished at the fact that how precisely her mental conclusions co-ordinated with the personality changes in Sly Fox, as she had christened Ridaline. It only elucidated the complementary nature of her rival- and the specificity. It looked like Mrs. Ridaline had started celebrating a non-stop party after a supposed win. She had become even more flagrantly garrulous and a complete social magnet- her friends and links might as well have called her 'a rising star', 'a gracious hostess'. Her face appeared fuller and she always looked to be pleasantly amused, except of course, in front of Skyra when she assumed a stern, tight-lipped attire. Her head stood a little taller than usual and her strides looked more energetic and definite. The phenomenon buzzed like fire emitting from a dragon and spread its waves in all directions.

But these vibrations ruffled Skyra. She didn't particularly like the undercurrent this shift of alignment brought with it. It was exactly the kind of background where she would never fit in. Nevertheless, the focus was created and it flourished head-on. There was the constant presence of some unaccounted fear palpable in the air that Skyra's stamina broke against. It was crippling; this exactly was the characteristic nature of the matter in question. All this was a bad signal-it held the promise of danger in it. It clearly suggested the gearing up to next advancing level- which appeared to be a sort of preparation for next attack. Skyra always went around wearing an invisible armour on her, but she found it stupid and most importantly, the restriction of her own mental freedom smothered her. She liked to live life like she didn't have a care in the world and this state of affairs had forced her to introspect. She had to find a way to blend with the winds of change-she had never shared such a subconscious relationship with anyone, she was sure it was closer than the relation Riddy shared with her husband.

Skyra did not look to have swallowed the potion well; on the contrary, she only seemed to be like her own reinforced version. The bar was raised, the distance widened. Riddy appeared to be possessed by a restless unidirectional force, she had a new mission to accomplish. Skyra, on the other hand, disciplined herself to live with it and found a solace in her endeavours. She had understood that she was being used as a central pillar to construct a web, as well as that she was unwanted- as a representative of something that needed to be squashed out of existence.

Skyra had had such enemies in the past, but how could one have a relation with someone one didn't talk to...?? She understood that the virulence potential was too high, the enemy was extremely talented and that the Krummers had been interested in her since beginning. She was being used as an experimental toy for their otherwise lacklustre life. It didn't go down well with her. She strived to find a remedy to spoil the show but for that she needed to go into details, the workings of Ridaline's mind. A psychological study. What makes her tick and how her system stands, blatant as it is. Only this knowledge would give her the taming power to tackle things that were spiralling out of her control. She wanted to know where their point in reality lay, if they really had a limit point? How much can one diverge from the realistic metaphysics, and get carried away? She was their anchor with reality, which they continuously tried to combat.

One thing was clear- the Krummers' efforts had lead them to transitionally create a fake imaginary world, which they kept on potentiating by their continuous efforts. It had become a sort of addictive drug for them weaning of which threatened their existence. This need drove them to consistently meet people and only when Riddy had thoroughly influenced them, she would have got her tonic. It was like keying plastic music-players, and the music that played would prove to provide the much-needed relief. All this formed a major part of Skyra's study on them. Skyra had found a way to thrive in her unsolved quest for mental peace, but the deepening of the darkness around her had an ominous sign.

Skyra knew Ridaline had been scrutinising her with a measuring stick. The woman was in control of the flow. One pull of the string would materialise any change she wished; all but on Skyra. She remained to be a persistent nuisance for her. She continued to look undisturbed, and though would look conscious of the surroundings, would never flinch a bit. The woman had swept her into a flurry, that was the only success till now but the bitter part was that Skyra seemed to have survived the attack.

Days had now turned into a challenge, and life into a battle-ground. The unacknowledged cold war now held its presence all the time, and now that Skyra turned out to be no naive duckling, Ridaline's willpower only grew stronger. She was analysing, waiting for the right time to drop the bomb-which seemed to be her hallmark. The woman kept expanding her horizons, so much so that it could neither be overcome nor be overlooked. Skyra felt her stature diminishing, which meant her nemesis had a much larger annexation to her credit by now. But Skyra always kept herself closed, not allowing any lid to remain open. She was safe, she thought.

Skyra had her injured self-esteem left with her. She had no idea which meadow her enemies were sending her to pasture-from where she stood, it was a dead-end if she didn't herself foray into the scheme of things. She had to find a solution to her unwarranted grievances and for that she had to take up the challenge. She too put out the all-stops in her manner with people. She let her inhibitions go away, and took the reins. All that mattered was to know she had control, it was a magnanimous undertaking and risky too, because people recognized her need to dominate. She made herself to be dramatic; she shrieked and gasped during her conversations. "The Great" head-turner was now opening up, all of a sudden, out of the blue, putting her self-esteem at stake, letting people have an insight into how normal she could be. Betty felt different-she didn't care to look for the reason, but she could see through the superfluous behaviour and instantly knew something had gone astray.

"Doesn't it bother you..? How she is acting up these days...? And they all seem to be giggling and laughing... having a good time...They are liking her…", asked her friend, Gina.

"You are an idiot, Gina", said Betty, filing her nails, not looking up.

"Exactly what do you mean...?"

"Can't you see how broken the mademoiselle is..?", she asked smugly.

Gina looked at her, perplexed, begging to explain.

"That is her 'denial behaviour' that she is carrying around. Did you ever think that snubbing bitch would ever care to mingle with riff-raff like us. You bet she hates it... The only reason is that she is sad...In other words, field day for us…."

Gina smiled, as her brain enlightened, grasping the hint like a radar.

"Decreased distance means increased exposure...We can certainly make use of it....Let's see her putting up a brave face...", Betty said.

She continued, "This is the right time for us to dig her wounds....This day had to come...The way the golden bird was flying, some plane had to hit her....Let's rise to the occasion..!! Our time has arrived!!"

The encounters were like passing through a ring of fire- the feat was completed, but there was always some amount of burns as a side-effect. For Skyra, the unfathomable chasm continued to broaden. She had had skirmishes with other women in life but never had it come to such serious terms that she felt herself destroyed. Every other tiff she had experienced before appeared to be miniscule and people she thought she hated before now appeared to be like twiglets. The never-ending, relentless, unstoppable havoc wrecked by her neighbour was stifling her. Riddy seemed to be like a bull on rampage, getting hungrier more and more with Skyra's safe perch. She seemed to be infuriated beyond her wits. The humiliation Skyra suffered last time had forced her to stretch her mental boundaries; she always made sure she was 10 steps ahead of Riddy. But Riddy showed an exceptional ability to compress herself in such situations. She would withdraw tightly into her shell like a snail, not allowing herself to touch the vibes sent off by Skyra's being, as if it burned on her skin. After manufacturing her own gases of vanity that clashed strictly against Skyra's harmonious world, she would let herself expand in the favourable condition that followed thereafter. Their auras had begun to clash with each other, and the flux was getting more and more tremendous day after day. Skyra had become sick of such exchange of energies-she could easily feel that she was the target of some missile directed specifically at her. With all her might, she tried to shun Ridaline from her thoughts, but her presence imposed like unwanted bog clinging to the feet. After a while, she gave up dwelling on such thoughts-they made her bitter. Once, she overheard the woman jabbering loudly to the plumber from her balcony. The voice was not just talking to the plumber, it was screaming out to everyone, making it known to one's senses of its presence- the shrill voice of a naughty leprechaun. It was like shots being fired to someone's ears. She had a way with words and could easily tame any person by it. Her thirst for people was getting insatiable. Skyra brooded bitterly over how the sympathy-generating woman had now worn the garb of a dictating leader; she looked swelled-up with a poisonous gas inside her that was a hair's breadth away from bursting out.

Riddy used to look at Skyra with accusing eyes. Skyra could easily see through the self-dignified facade but did not counter back. She accepted it all, very innocently. The encounters always had the quality of interrupting the normal flow of moment, which would otherwise have been. They were like electricity flowing in the wire, which was impeded and returned back through some alternative route without completing the circuit. A repelling unagreed ground always prevailed. The percussions were revolting.

Skyra had become sure of the woman's 'psychopathicness' and knew that Ridaline probably thought about her all the time-her imaginary world was hinged at Skyra's defeats. It had started to put her off. Many times, it used to be clear that the woman had been desperate to see her, to know how much still good she was and secondly, to execute her desired effect on Skyra. Ridaline's existence had become like an irritating fly one desperately wanted to get rid of but couldn't because of the fly's dexterity. Skyra contemplated further playing with the mind-the woman was spreading herself multi-directionally, but Skyra's non-participation was now making her look like a peaked loser. She had started to lose her effect. So in order to turn things around, she too started banging her door to convey messages of hatred and of rebellion. It gave her a teeny-weeny headway and some much-needed space in the subconscious pool that seemed to be drowning her, but only a fleeting satisfaction. The abstract race continued, till Skyra was beginning to taste the freedom that she had been longing to have back again. She thought she was a free bird again- free from any mental torsions, and that no force tough enough to reckon with her existed. Her experimentation had eventually born fruits.

Riddy was inside her room, pacing to and fro furiously. She had flung down the phone after sternly talking to the customer care official from the bank. "Damn these suckers...!!! Why do they have to call to irritate me...!! He knew that it was a bad time, so that bastard called now!!! And he was laughing at me from the other end, enjoying!!!"

She took the remote and started toggling the channels. Then she turned the television off and threw the remote across. The moments were getting difficult to pass.

"It's her!! It's her! She is doing this to me....She has made a fool of me...That little smartass has slipped right through my fingers...It wasn't such a cakewalk as it looked to be... That cute monster is turning out to be a pain in the neck... Giving me such a hard time...So she thinks she has won? Wait till she gets this....I will send the world crashing down on her....I will make her say 'yes' to being my slave....until she cringes and yelps like a puppy....", she mumbled through a dangerous twist of lips.

I WANT HER INSIDE MY FIST!!!!, she screamed.... "This is my dream...I rule the world by ruling on her...If the heroine says "Surrender", the power automatically comes into my hands...Such a direct method......Bault, why doesn't that dummy get it?? She will hand me that honour herself...I will make her!! I am the empress of the world... How dare that demon give me such a hard time...?? I will get into the deepest corner of her brain and eat her inside out...I will go to any length to see that look on her face....That's all I want and I will have it, by hook or by crook!!! Bault...where the hell are you???"

CHAPTER 7

FANTASY

She felt sick. She felt like a trapped prisoner. "This kind of world can't exist...!! It's a lie....!! It's presence is a sham...!!!" She drew a step back, and looked all around her- at the animated faces of the people as if enacting a movie. She felt herself breaking down, unable to accept. She had never faced such a situation in her life before, in the challenges she tackled during her reign. One could fight if a comprehensible problem exists, then work out the solution, one could fight a battle if there was actually a battle, but this....It was like a shapeless messy pulp which had no definitions, how did one ever grapple with a thing like that?...She did not know what the problem was, she had never asked or wished for this kind of boggling dilemma. She felt weak and helpless. The picture of the woman flashed before her eyes....

"A flower like you will be crushed, and every time I succeed, the world will be coloured in my hue, more and more..."

She carried herself to a rock and sat down on it.

"I will change the face of this earth forever....."

The words were pounding on her ear-drums.

"In place of it, will rise a country ruled by me, people burning their blood and sweat to worship me....And-"

No, you won't-Skyra cried. And I won't let you....I will never ever accept this....I don't know what you are doing or how you are doing, but I will find a way around it. A country with you as the Countess- the whole idea appeared preposterous....It is not staying for long...With Skyra bowing down to her- it was something Skyra could laugh all day about. Skyra felt a sense of rebellion rising in her, warrior. All she knew that she had to go back; she had been beginning to feel too "home-sick". Steeling her bearings, she rose. She didn't realise, but she had been shaking her head in vehement disapproval.

An old hunchback lady with greying knotted hair, walking with a stick was speaking to her through blackened teeth:

"Her Majesty is the kindest person on earth. May her legacy live on forever...!!! Don't you think?"

She turned to look at her, but Skyra was gone. She knew that she had to fight her toughest battle yet. She felt a lot better, now that the decision had clearly been formed in her mind. She also understood what undertaking such a task implied. But she had to take up the challenge; it seemed to be the most practical thing to do. She had to trust her own instincts, follow her own verdict. There was no one to seek, to hold on to. The whole thing centered on her- and she knew it. In the scheme of things where she stood, though it seemed the downright craziest thing to try to break the indomitable, it was also the only way left to fight. She was the one put into the tight spot, no one would understand so vividly as she did. And even if they did, they wouldn't know what to say except the right things. It was her problem and she had to solve it herself. Her nerve had been touched-there was no denying it. And then it was clear as a crystal to her that the authority lay on her; if she wouldn't grant the permission, this stinking world won't stand. She would permanently wipe it out, she needed to go deep down to its roots. And to get down to the roots, she needed to play, as the woman had said. Self-defence was not her only aim, it aroused pity; destruction was becoming her motto. Every sort of evil can be tackled, her father had said.

She had been attacked unprepared, this was the true nature of devil. She needed to beef up her senses, gather up and store energy for the coming days, which would be anything but hard. Diamond cuts diamond, iron cuts iron and shrewdness cuts shrewdness. She had to prepare herself to be bad-it would be her new cross-identity from now on. And she had to teach herself how to carry it well. And that it should remain hidden, and not spill over to other people's view. The quality of her enemy, she had to ingrain into her own being-that was the only weapon as of now. An alter-ego. She will learn to masquerade, to put on an act for her own sake. For her battle. It had started to mean a lot to her already. She had to learn to hold out time, which was the only factor keeping her behind. She was unknown to fear; but unless she would crack the nut, fear will be allowed to run scot-free. She had to prepare herself to see things that one doesn't like, at the same time loathing it, knowing it as wrong and yet not being able to counter it because a remedy is still being awaited. That precisely, would be the most nerve-wracking part, demanding patience beyond limit. And the game had just yet started.

She was walking, enraged, cutting through the trees and bushes, her surroundings invisible to her. The place did not pinch her any longer. She felt natural, at-home.

And it was then that she had reached the Bloomburg Palace.

CHAPTER 8

REALITY

It took some time for Skyra to get accustomed to the new mood that filled the air. She felt like she had lost her footing for a second, but staggered back to her position. But the new stance did not exactly match her original one-there were some voids. She felt that a piece of her backbone were lacking. She made up for the gaps it by means of conquering other people. For the first time in her life, she had felt the necessity to fake herself-she knew that it was an excuse to keep her broken pieces together. Seldom, she would feel compassion for herself, she wondered if she was pitiable. She didn't feel as blessed to be herself as she did before. Her joyous flame had been near extinguishment, and now she was busy building a shield to protect it further. Never before, she had felt so exposed in life. She had lost the pleasure of living in the moment. Though she did not falter at work, the rampwalks felt monotonous, she felt the need of a greater challenge with a greater thrill. Her walk had undergone a change; her ankles did not thump down with the spunk as they did earlier, they undulated with the fluidity of a thick liquid. When she would walk down, she felt her head floating in an ocean; her face had lost the angles and looked rounder.

"You know Skyra, you are not being yourself these days... Is this a permanent change....??", asked Betty, cornering her alone.

"So you are the change inspector now...??", asked Skyra.

"What I mean is....U never behaved this way before.... You know, like one of us....Is everything alright...??", Betty said. "I was just a little concerned."

Skyra laughed. "What else......??"

"You have kept your friends close, but never your enemies closer..."

"Well, you have bridged the gap, haven't you...??"

Bault was happy under the shadow of Ridaline. He had never before felt so self-satisfied, like a complete man. There had always been some unreachable depths before which he could never explain, but now things were different. Ridaline had lost her stiffness and always made him feel light and easy. Perhaps, she had instilled a maturity in their relationship which they both took as a welcome change; he felt confident and fresh most of the time. He felt himself slightly honoured to be her husband and the way she gelled with the guests, literally had him jumping on the sofa cushions. People at office had asked him the cause of his recently-found fulfilment and he would be tempted to answer "my wife". He was aware that he needed her more than she needed him. She had always been the leader out of the two, giving him the proper guidance and helping him make decisions, when he clammed up. To speak the truth, he felt lost and incomplete without her. He was thankful to her to make up for his own shortcomings, and for that reason he considered her the supreme woman in his life. And now that she understood him so deeply, he did not need a soul near him. His respect for her had grown tremendously and even though she had lost her temper unreasonably once or twice and lashed out more than necessary, he had compromised whole-heartedly. He felt glad that they were going great, mutually and socially. She would call up at office and he would listen to her voice which sounded melodious than ever. They went out frequently, trying to match the frequency of the world against theirs, glad that it looked so small from where they stood.

Skyra thought that she had been born only to be slaughtered at the hands of that woman. Her whole life had been a part of some counterfeit peep show, a complete fiasco. Now overshadowed by a looming apocalypse, what if she was sucked into it completely and irredeemably; it made her shiver sometimes.

All this had forced Skyra to don a new personality outwardly. She learnt to carry herself in a self-contained manner lest her "light be stolen." It offered her the immunity from being martyred again and again, and also helped her put Riddy in dark circles about her calibre. It was a skill that she had bartered from her. Later on, she would release herself. It was like a deploy. It was taxing nevertheless- it stressed her out. But this suppression was essential to create the optical illusion-the very method through which she had been tricked. A great part of her surface protective layers had been torn apart to leave her core exposed, which she had to protect, and for which a suitable defence mechanism was needed. Her rival had an unusual expertise in distorting reality and sweeping people into the vanity-rich current. Her style and mannerisms appealed to the most 'inferior' morals in a man, calling it out to rise from the crevices and come into action. She was too busy constructing a dirty mesh consisting of dark and impotent heaviness that acted as a blow to any happy free person, and asking him to join. Riddy would not step back even a tad, neither would Skyra tolerate all of this. Therefore, with each and every passing day, the psychological time of the two got connected. Now, Ridaline's presence had become vicious enough to mimic the effect of black-hole, sucking all light and energy into itself.

CHAPTER 9

FANTASY

"Has something happened dear..??", Aunt asked her one evening. She had long been wishing to bring up this question since quite a few days, but had been wondering if it was the right thing to ask.

"No....nothing. Why, does it look like...??", Skyra asked casually, throwing the matter out of the window.

Aunt could not stop but notice that Skyra looked serious these days, as if she was working her mind on some important question. Her air of vulnerability was gone and she looked uptight, all of which was not customary to her. She did not look cheerful very often. She did not laugh at things she was expected to and seemed drawn in her own world. She had started talking straight-to-the-point which was actually typical of her, but only this time her replies would seem to leave an unfilled gap hanging in the air. She would talk and give the proper comments, but they were not vivacious enough. Once when Skyra was looking into her eye, she had felt the presence of something not present physically, but having an importance, which can't be undermined. She could not give a voice to her words, she had been afraid to speak to herself but was she losing interest in things? Either this or the other inference which she preferred to believe that she was turning into a woman, the maturity she had been missing had finally sprung into her. Or was it just a passing phase?

"Not literally, but as a matter of fact....", she replied, casting her thoughts aside.

"Say Aunt, am I contemptible...??", Skyra asked, tilting her head to one side.

"In....what....sense...."

"In the sense that I make other women feel small and ugly, wouldn't that be absolutely unethical on my part...?? Haven't you ever felt jealous of me, Aunt Madeline...?"

"Huh....?"

"Come on....I really want to know....", Skyra said with heightened alertness. The mockery lay in the fact that she was serious.

"Once....It was Annual Prestoria Day....You were 15, and it was the first time you came in like a lady, in your mother's gown...The whole crowd was enticed with you... They couldn't believe what they saw, they would turn their heads and look again.... "The princess is beautiful, "they seemed to be saying-no, their eyes said that....Even the remarks were underscoring....They were swarming to you like moth to flame...Harold was the happiest father on earth....I confess, for a second, I had the feeling if I too had possessed the radiance you have....But you are unique.... Everybody can't be the same, we are all different...."

"I remember," Skyra said wistfully, "But did you feel like killing me...??"

"Hell, no...!! Where do you get such crazy ideas from? What matters is that I was proud to be your Aunt... Everything else is sidelined..."

"What makes us different...?"

"How on earth am I supposed to know...??", she shrugged.

"You know, they say there might be multiple universes out there....Isn't it just like us? Each of us lives in a world of our own, which we prefer to believe and create it the way we might want it to be....And when people meet, the universes they represent collide with each other and then they are merged or twisted or disfigured.....and sometimes collapsed.....And we wish that if they were all synchronous entities rather than all of them with different frequencies.... sometimes completely out of tune with each other, it would be much nicer...."

"You're being too pessimistic....Every person is not each other's enemy...Afterall, we all want to live in peace and harmony....Even if there is a war, in the end we all concede...", Aunt Madeline said.

"And what about those that go on endlessly....till eternity??"

"There's only one kind...those between good and evil..."

Skyra nodded. "Do people come with good or evil labelled on them...??"

"It's a personal matter of the individual...A choice that our mental faculty makes..."

"So you mean to say what might be good for me, might be evil for you...and vice-versa...??"

"Yes...But the situation becomes different if one compromises......"

"Even though it crushes you inside...?"

"In that case, the best answer is no...We should only accept as much as our heart can take...."

"I know the bacteria now, Aunt.....", she whispered inaudibly under her breath.

She had vowed she would never ever have to visit that land again. She would not allow herself to be a part of it, she won't touch it. She kept going as usual, immersing herself in her daily duties, attending her courtly responsibilities, it gave her pleasure-it was like surging through hurdles. At the end of the day, she slept a satisfied sleep.

Far away in Helfung, Countess Ridaline was glancing at the final blocks of stones being put into their right places. "Superb", she smiled. "Let the preparations begin". She giggled maliciously.

Chapter 10

REALITY

Ridaline glanced furtively at the clock on the mantle-piece. It was time, she thought. The butterflies in her stomach won't let her keep still. She looked at Bault across the room- she saw approval. It was Doomsday. The excitement enthused in them knew no bounds.

It was around 6:30 pm. The sun looked blood orange from the window of the metro train. The air was light and crispy. Skyra smiled at the small boy sitting across the aisle, clutching a Pokémon card tightly in his fingers. She was glad to feel that even after all the unprecedented things happening in her life, she could still let positivity get the better of her.

All she remembered of the meeting with the Krummers that evening was that their cold certainty resembled that of zombies rising out of graveyards.

Chapter 11

FANTASY

The prison had two walls, slanting to meet towards the top, while the third side was a grilled window revealing the sun and the sea. Skyra awoke to discover her left wrist was shackled. She heard the thunderous music of the drums coming from below. It was followed by the roar of the crowd. If the sound were transformed into a picture, it would resemble the wide-open jaw of a crocodile, baring its jagged teeth.

Was it the rock-bottom of her life, she asked herself. She laughed bitterly at the remarkable irony that her nadir coincided with the zenith of the Krummers.

She let a finger drag on the surface of the floor. She recoiled.

(It was the swearing-in ceremony of the Count, who had assumed the position of Commander-in-chief.)

CHAPTER 12

REALITY

It was like being passed a death sentence and facing the guillotine. But the satirical thing was that the judge and the criminal had exchanged places. Every sound sounded different, every touch was strange and every sight appeared creepy. Time stood still. It could go on and on and still feel the same. Maybe, the earth had stopped spinning. The headache won't go. It was like caught in a time warp. Or cursed into stagnancy. This is what people mean when they say the end of the world. A dead-end was reached and there was no way back. She felt like being used as a tool to accomplish a long-ranged mission. There were drumrolls into the creation of a new world. The world has now gone into evil hands and she can do nothing about it. She felt invisible concrete walls blocking her that seemed to scorn the fists that broke helplessly on it. All she knew was that now, her life would be changed forever. Her head felt like it was buried under a ton of bricks, tied in knots. It was caged. A giant tornado had broken all thresholds and seeped into every nook and cranny of her brain.

"This was only half of it, the next half will be written by me and I will have it back what you took from me. What you think you have permanently, is just on hold until I finish the game you started and don't complain if you get hurt in the process...Don't celebrate yet...The game is extended, with my terms and my rules, and you don't have any option but to continue playing, which you will and you have to....Either I will knock you down or you will be left in limbo, but you will not get the joy of victory....Now I will drive home the point in your way, the only language which will work...I always waited for your maximum, this was it....And now I am free to reply you back, to put my skills to action...You have given me the prerogative by giving me all the reason in the world, by toeing the line first....And I am glad for it...So this was all it had to come down to?.... It is only now that I am actually starting to take you in the serious manner as you have been taking me....

"So I am that important to you?...I have not yet gotten into the attacking-zone yet...You thought this was bad?... Wait till you see what bad actually is....Let me get into my actual villain mode, you will see for yourself and I challenge you to raise yourself to that level too...There would be no justifications, plain battle...No-holds-barred manner....All those feelings I had been having a hard time suppressing, will come out especially for you as a treat...In full explosion...Let's see how far your road leads you now.... You will be punished beyond any hope in hell...I was the victim hitherto, now I am your contender....I don't know the consequences, but I will foil your plans for tomorrow...I will fight till I break...The paradox of your world is that it stands on a foundation of nothing, other than the hollowness of your own souls....It has a limited shelf-life...Let you people be the example of a living proof...Hell hath no fury like a woman scorned...."

So this was the end they wanted to reach- a shortcut to reach the top through a single person, by short-circuiting the normal way in which they have bleak chances to succeed, plus the excitement trimmed...Destroying her peace to establish superiority in their otherwise decadent world... She realised she will have to change herself...bring out the bad in her in full throttle...There was no way she could put her indignation under wraps anymore...She would withdraw her sanction, and not only that, she would now encourage them to take her as a heavy adversary, this time openly and without pretence....In an open playing field....They had shifted the goalposts, but she couldn't change her pavilion... The gravity of the matter had abrupted the flow of signal in the neurones of her brain...Now it was her turn to be the life-sucker....The peace-destroyer...The black sheep discontent with the picture....It was getting on her nerves....

There was a great deal of rebuilding and regeneration to do...Bloodshed....Right, the face of the earth would be changed forever....it will have a scar etched on it right across...and everything will be rewritten.....

It was 9 a.m. when Skyra was looking in the mirror. Her face looked exactly like it looked 10 years ago, in middle-school. She was amazed at how she had went through a wormhole and awakened back in that era, still stepping in the adult world, learning the thicks and thins of life. She felt as if she were outside her body, a distant person observing her face, a different person. Then her thought diverted to the apartment next door, and what she felt towards herself was abhorrence. She cancelled her shows for the coming week.

First, she had to figure out a way to get out of this abstract mess. She knew that these kinds of consequences happened, but only when someone hands the other the insights into their mind. She had learnt by experience long ago the art of keeping her boundaries latched, so no one would get permitted entry. People called her introvert and reserved. But how much more closed could she possibly keep herself? It was like some person with X-ray glasses were penetrating her whole mind with the map laid out clearly before her. She knew the only way to outsmart her rival was by misleading, in such a case, if Riddy saw everything so well. She prepared herself to grow fond of the woman she despised, to embrace the torture and feel the sacrilege to be a purifying act; to like the unpleasantness. The woman was desperate to get attention and carve out a considerable niche for herself, now Skyra would offer the whole world to be hers....She would actually step down her own throne and offer the bridle to her hands, which she had anyway snatched from her...Instead of direct rebelling, she would make herself dysfunctional outwardly to see how much her world proliferates; how the world under evil power, temporarily though, appears...combined with it her own subduction feels...She wanted to test herself against it, to see how much more can she take....If it had to happen, if it was in her destiny to go through this, why not each and every bit of it, instead of a trifling glimpse....Her open retaliation this time would give Riddy insurmountable pleasure.... Skyra had a bad time accepting that she was the deflated loser once again....But if Riddy wanted her to be tiny in stature and made that possible, why not?....She wondered if she were living nearby a borderline psychopath, who gambled on people to target her.

She needed a deeper connection with her, the thing which she shunned away from, would now be her biggest asset. Let the obvious apply itself in practice. Now she never shuddered when she got a hinting sound of them coming or going; instead she would deliberately cross her 'limiting' line and step into the balcony to see either of them; she wanted to downplay the fear by facing it. Not a day went without an encounter. This happened several times too soon. At first, it miffed Ridaline to think that Skyra's guts had soared high-instead of lying in some corner of her apartment, she had rebounded. But on the other side, it also made her happy to think that it meant Skyra now probably thought about her more intensely than before-a clear sign how deep her effects had sunk, and her meticulous potions had worked and that it can't be undone ever-the biggest milestone was reached, permanently. She was glad beyond words to think that she clouded her subconscious; the rabbit was finally inside the snare.

It was life-altering. Skyra's whole life had come to an unanticipated standstill unless she would find a way to solve the puzzle –if she wouldn't, it would brand her life as a failure. She would have to burrow out a crack by starting somewhere; she would have to take risks, create entirely new original paths and sweep the course in her direction. She was lagging far behind, and felt as small as the granules of salt are compared to an ocean. She was amused to find herself in such a meagre position, swearing and cursing, or that she would ever feel so strongly about a person, be affected by a person to such an extent that she would have to plan and plot the course of her relations with other people. She guessed it was contagiousness from Riddy.

Unequivocally, the Krummers were the active obstacles in her present life-and they were very well aware and cherished the fact. Nobody Skyra had met before had presented such irreducible intricacies, or evoked such strong reactions in her body and mind. She had to cross over it, or it would prey on her, torment her for the rest of her life that she didn't try. It would be like walking on a double-edged sword, she can harm herself even more by actively participating and exposing herself, but she didn't care- all that mattered was to break the norms. The rest will automatically follow, it will be all new and unseen and surprising; she wanted it to transcend to the highest level by releasing the pressure-valve. She would turn her enemy into the very instruments of play that they had been using her for.

The eye-contacts that followed thereafter only supported Skyra's conjecture. Skyra's rays were lost on her and Ridaline looked more expressive and uninhibited than ever-a concentrated ball of negativity. The meetings disgusted her even more. It was then that it occurred to Skyra that she was missing something in the riddle. It was the husband. She was surprised that she had forgotten about him altogether. That now, the sensitive site of attack was him- he was acting as the boundary wall that deflected everything. He had been possessed last time and took the centrestage willingly, owning up to show his allegiance to Ridaline's rule. A perfect pawn to fulfil his wife's purpose.

Skyra thought she can expand her frontiers by including him in the game, which he secretly was, by using his acceptance of contempt for her.

For the next two days, Skyra lived in an inferno- pinned at the sole hope of an encounter with the husband, the person who will take the bullet and in turn, release her.

It was like to move around with a grindstone tied around her leg. It was the end of the universe, she felt like watching the earth from a point high above in the stratosphere, from a satellite and pondered how small she were. A rush of adrenaline would slosh in her stomach and go back downwards. A packet of energy wiggling to get out of her but couldn't but at the right time-the point unreached. Her face was drained of colour, she looked downcast, sucked of brightness. Riddy was happy that she had sent the bitch on exile, closing in on her from all sides, by a single move of making Bault feel he is the king of the world.

The show next day seemed to be a Herculean task. Somehow, she made herself cover the distance to Elysee Avenue and made it to the fashion house. The hall was bustling with people. Everything going was routine as usual, only today it seemed to be chaotic and full of frenzy. It all seemed to be hanging in between, with no beginning and no end. But when she talked to people, she fully grasped the state of her mind. She realised she had to hold herself together till the end of the show. Then she would be back home. She knew her face was blank and devoid of life; she felt like an alien from some other planet, observing things for the first time. The world seemed too much for her, she could not handle it anymore. She might as well have been a baby, who had to learn every lesson all over again. She was not the same Skyra anymore, everything had been ruined. This was the worst- not knowing where it is going, everything caught in an eddy, pulling it round and round with no end. She thought with terror if she was losing her mind. She silenced and told herself that it was okay. That she knew where to go and what to do- it was just the wait which was terribly excruciating.

She had to pull herself together and take one step at a time. This was also worst part-this state of suppressed existence, a dam holding all the force back, and only one button that would let go of it. That barring stop had to be removed, at any cost, by any means, as soon as possible. Then she relaxed and tried to tell herself that it will be, she only needed some amount of patience. But then, the horrendous would occur to her-if she were caught in this whirlpool forever. And she would feel the pain jabbing her inside again. She glanced at her cell phone-it had only been 30 minutes, it felt like 3000 years. Thrown back to the beginning, before civilizations, to the formation of the universe before any war had been fought, if she would not succeed, all the wars that were fought and prevailed by good would lose their meaning. The world would exist no longer, but as an empty platform, empty of love.

She knew she had been split into two- and one part remained far behind the other. It had to catch up with the other or she won't suffice. It was a wrecking struggle, like attempting to mimic the speed of light, to escape reality because it was too painful. She closed her eyes and heard her heartbeat-she knew she still had a chance. She knew it would leave bad memories, but whoever cared for such trivialities. When she chose the path she would take, she was aware of its arduosity; she could not go back now, neither could she give in. She knew it was a thin and narrow and tortuous path that she would have to scrape through, that it would extract a lot of energy, only she had not known it would hurt this much. There was no other option but to face it, in its full-blown picture. It was difficult, she wondered how much more difficult it would be. A fierce force, intent and hell-bent on stopping her. Now she was getting a taste of two forces, united for a single cause. The scene that rose before her portrayed how the world will appear if she were eliminated from it, except that she was physically present, yet witnessing her negation, her contribution notwithstanding. She had taken a backseat, like a compressed spring, storing all the elastic energy inside. Her frame of mind was completely out of sync with that of the people around her, like two circles just touching each other eccentrically. Try as she might, she could not bring it to juxtapose it in correct order. It was mayhem-she could not endure it any longer. Then she convinced herself it was temporary- just this day, or a few more.

She avoided conversation with everybody. The show seemed to be the least important thing on earth. She did not feel different from others, as she had always felt. She was just one of the average girls, living in the flurry of the moment. Her deep-seated composure was gone. The crowd was smothering her, layering her with a coat that won't let her move an inch. She was aware of the fact that she was pushing too hard, hopelessly trying to break the dam, in futile. She did not remember when she festooned the runway, it was too easy. She left in a jiffy. She returned back to the nail-biting turmoil in her apartment. The day wound up without any change. It was extremely hard to bear the state of things as they were, when she knew she possessed the potential to upturn it her way. With each passing day, the heaviness accumulated in her head doubled exponentially.

Skyra was numb from being stuck in a mental labyrinth. But when she finally had a chance to see Bault Krummer face to face, she felt a quintal of burden lifting off her shoulders. The floodgates had been opened.

Chapter 13

FANTASY

The shackles had given way to set her hand free. Gently, she rose and walked towards the window to face the navy blue sky. She punched it with one fist; the grill shattered to pieces. Standing on the edge, she heaved a deep breath of air into her lungs and somersaulted into the chilly water down below. She swam a moderate distance, about ten yards when she reached an aggregation of rocks. Memories of her younger days flashed before her eyes, when she used to swim in the lake, tame horses like a man until a bump on the knee hurled her back to the present. She held on to a half-submerged rock and propped herself up on it. She ran her hand on her knew and felt blood spouting. The crescent moon looked serene, but its ends fatally sharp. She was back into the water, clenching her teeth. About half an hour later, her muscles fatigued, she reached the shore. It was past midnight, pitch black; the sand felt warm and welcoming with arms wide open. She gulped bouts of air of freedom; but all she knew was that she had not yet escaped this land.......

She saw a spot of fire in the far distance; it started moving towards her. She gasped and ran head over heels. She had lost her shoes in the sea and tripped over and fell. When she looked behind, the light had approached nearer, it looked bigger. She panicked. She did not want to go back to the prison. Amidst the consternation, she started to lose her balance. The long swim to the beach had drained her of all energy, she was as much as just chugging along. A sturdy hand gripped her forearm firmly, the hand of a man. He stared at her longer than necessary.

She could make out his face in the illumination of the lantern.

"Come with me", he said. She did not know if he was requesting her, or ordering her. Her first impulse was to look at the vast space lying ahead of her, but she was weak and vagabond and she found herself giving in.

He did not speak to her the entire time; she did not know whether to trust him or take him as an enemy, but there was a definite finality in his style, a sharpness that reminded her of nobody else but herself. He had left her hand, she could run if she pleased, but she decided against it.

It was a small hut, made of hay and wood. When she stepped inside, she brought with her the water dripping off her sodden dress. Now she could see him entirely, his full features- thick eyebrows, a lofty nose and tight-set lips. He was looking at a point between her collar bone and navel; she felt half abashed and half offended.

"You better get out of your clothes", he said, "It will increase your hypothermia".

He walked up to a wooden chest kept in the corner and squatted down to reach inside it. He threw a fur-sheet on the cot and went outside with the lantern. He did not show up again. Skyra shrugged and peeked outside. She saw his silhouette drifting away. She closed the door stealthily behind her. Then she slipped out of her dress and unfurled the sheet. She used it as a blanket; the warmth perfusing into her skin. She felt safely wrapped in comfortable nest and wafted into an intoxicating sleep.

She was woken up by shuffling noise coming from inside the room. She sat up instantaneously, startled, exposing her breasts; saw him and quickly lied down again.

"How did you get inside...?", she asked in anger.

"I knocked, but you were fast asleep...In case you noticed, there is another door which I keep locked from outside", he said. She felt even more outraged to see the hint of a faint smile on his face. But to her ultimate dismay, she found herself ogling his figure in turn.

"I think my dress is dry now...Mind if you leave me alone for a while..?"

"Certainly......", he said and obeyed after unlatching the door.

She quickly put on her outfit and stepped outside into the bright luminescent sunlight. It felt so wonderful to feel the light all over again, to be free and without a care; she stayed, drinking in the warmness of the atmosphere. Then her gaze flitted to the blue sea and she felt both happy and sad. The nightmare was over.

"I feel stuck here", she said.

"Me too", he replied. It was unexpected, what he said and she was not sure he meant what she thought he meant.

"What do you mean...?", she asked, bewildered.

"Same as you do...", he replied.

"How did you know?", she asked.

He shrugged and said: "I am from Slakevo….It was annexed by Helfung; it doesn't exist anymore……What happened last night?"

"It's a long story...So you actually believe this, all of it?", she asked.

"If I did, we won't be having this conversation", he said plainly.

She nodded. "But what about others...Have you met anybody who has spoken your thoughts..?"

"Actually, I did….Last night…You…."

She ignored the answer and said: "They have fallen for it. Their minds have given way...They aren't astute enough to make out the difference..."

"So you are on a mission to straighten out the mess by making them understand..?", he said, moving to gather some dry leaves and branches.

"That is out of the question. But there might be an alternative way...But, are we the only ones who can see what they can't...?"

He paused. "What?"

"The shift of equilibrium."

The young man prepared tea on the fire kindled on the twigs and offered her a cup, himself having one.

Suddenly, she said: "It's all because of me..."

She narrated her captivity in prison and her escape from it last night.

"So you see, with my vanquishment bit by bit, Ridaline will get stronger and more powerful. That is her sole aim- to capture me forever. She will move mountains if required. But she will do it, nonetheless. That is the exact reason of everything spiralling out of control. And that I don't know how to solve it...I am doing the best to my level..."

"Why did you let her do this to you...?"

"It's her methods...I can't match them...Human fear is making her do wonders... That's the difference...But I am taking a leaf from each lesson learnt..."

"It's not difficult to imagine you both as rivals...", he commented.

Her eyes moistened. She was gazing at a fixed point on the ground.

"What's the matter?", he asked.

"At one time, I used to think I was the luckiest girl in the world".

"Don't lose heart. You will escape, like I will. We are together in it...My name is Henry..."

"Skyra....Queen of Prestoria...."

CHAPTER 14

REALITY

Though the clouds were clearer the next day, Ridaline's tempers flared big time. The effect that was prohibited from pervading its known receptor-zone had crawled inside through Bault. Skyra had known that faking was easy, but nobody could be so impermeable. *Paper tiger*, she said to herself. He had the guts to abet Riddy's conquests, now he had to take the bullet for her.

Neither Skyra could nor she would ever try to justify herself or take one in her team, but she could do one thing-be at loggerheads with the one who has himself chosen to join and brazenly flaunt her opponent's team. Skyra would never be the fool to try to disengage the pull of mental control Riddy had on him, and last time only exemplified the level to which his faculties were corrupted. Moreover, his own accordance could not be denied-they had something in common, vanity, which talked greatly to him. He had simplified it for her-she was thankful. It was important. Earlier, by being in the shadows, he was on a comparatively safer ground. But his open declaration had changed all equations, ousted Skyra; so she felt irreproachably clear.

The theory and application tallied each other, perfectly. He had to come square with the discrepancies that entailed his open admittance. If his addition could multiply the effects, it could also act as a damper. Ridaline was stumped, her eyes widened beyond normal measures; but her manners showed she would have her way still, she seemed desperate to show her undeterrence and ready to take on the rest. "Bring it on", she seemed to shout. Her volume was expanding, and it was clear to Skyra that she was searching for a space to dig her dagger in to get even. The sunlight seemed too loud, as though they were reflecting back the repercussions sent by the clashing of the two forces; everything appeared to be stretched beyond their normal meaning, into an ulterior significance. The aftershocks in Riddy won't subside; she continued to act in a hysterical way, as if she had just discovered that her fortune has been forfeited.

She was shocked to see how her perfect state had been thrown in a state of disorder. The knowledge that how easily prone she was by prodding in through her most resilient weapon (which now also proved to be her biggest weakness) was too hard to swallow. That Skyra would use Bault to her own advantage like this-as a doorway into her otherwise 'fool-proof' world. Yet this time, instead of heeding the warning, she swelled to double her stride. Skyra found her presence stubborn and this behaviour sickening, like she was acting up for some unequalled throne. It only threw light on the lack of class; and illusion of intellect; and the darkness of mind.

"It's me, so it's okay...I can take care of myself...Had it been someone else, it would have been too damaging...But then, all this won't be happening if it were not me....", Skyra concluded.

She decided to stay in seclusion for the coming days in order to put an abrupt stop to her unending mental stalking; secondarily, it would also give her a breather (from the war) to wash off all the dirtiness she had been exposed to. She did not know whether to laugh or cry at the roller-coaster ride her life was shoving her through.

After precisely 8 days, when Skyra was sure that she had made her rival fall a considerable distance behind, she decided to survey the scenario-hoping that her rival had calmed down, but to no avail. When she made her presence, hatching out of her shell, she was flabbergasted to discover that Ridaline was still pursuing her-her sharp glance made Skyra conscious of her own outline. It was like passing under the metal scanner to detect residual strength, a tad here and a smattering there, in the angular flex of her knee and the twist of her ankle.

Riddy had no individual separate life of her own, and had resolved to align it in parallel with Skyra's; first Skyra had to be done away with, the rest of the world came later. Skyra's key-strategy was to make Riddy realise that she would never be getting rid of her, that she was unbreakable and that one could humour oneself by trying till infinity- in short, that it was impossible...like breaking the law of gravity. It was clear from looking at Ridaline that Skyra now represented nothing, what with the wimping out for a week-it had a sort of triumphant gloating in it. Riddy thought- the rat is finally out of its spider-hole, thinking the coast is clear. The iron was hot. It was time. Riddy was just one step away from victory, soon she will be ready to hoist the flag. Skyra knew that Riddy can't bear the sight of her free-minded, without Riddy hovering over her mind; that Ridaline couldn't be able to sit still, she had to do something to up the ante. These were the points, Skyra kept counting them, when one has the option to choose which way to go, it lay in one's own hands; when one could retreat back, or tread further down the road and tarnish one's soul even greater extent. She knew her enemy too well to even joke about stepping back. Such opportunities filled Riddy with excitement. The drumrolls had again begun.

It was the first time a person was going on berserk, flouting all rules, undoing all barriers- in abstraction, of course. What had intrigued Skyra about the whole issue was the fact that her enemy was resilient enough to put forth all her might in it; it was the most brow-raising and the disturbing fact of the matter. It affected her, pulled Skyra into it and also held a corollary-derived conclusion- that the more important Skyra was to her (as a part of a personal battle close to heart), more Riddy was susceptible too to be broken down, if her dream was thwarted. It had now unquestionably become the biggest quagmire and challenge of Skyra's life. The cat and mouse game won't let up.

Next day was accepted to be crucial day- a tie-breaker. It held the vibrations to break fresh ground. When Skyra made her appearance, fully charged-Riddy quickly rushed inside. Skyra kept sipping her coffee from the mug, perched on her chair, waiting for the show to unfold. Riddy noticed the speed in her limbs had increased than yesterday, transgressing the margins of her best-laid tactics.

Skyra heard a bang of the door, then noises down the stairs; Riddy was wearing a skirt, something she hadn't seen her in before. She stood straight, facing her directly opposite, like a conqueror assessing the looted treasure, which henceforth will bear a tag to his name. It was not just that, she seemed to be screaming it to her face that she has done it, achieved it finally. For the first time, Skyra felt like a judge, that it was important for her to acknowledge her defeat herself, that they didn't know if they had succeeded, that the satisfaction won't come if she didn't. But Skyra's face showed something else. She had always evaded eye-contacts, but this time she would use it as an opportunity to her advantage. Her temper knew no limits, she stared deep into Ridaline's eyes along her line of vision, diving inside, crashing the hurdles out of the way until she reached a tough core which wouldn't allow any further entry. She was aware that this was a priceless chance, when the enemy had indicated interest; she had to make the predator the prey; that she had to make her point hit home. In one protrusion of her eye, the rope with the hook attached was flung and the anchor established. She had touched that point and advanced far beyond that. It would show its effects steadily-like a forest fire.

CHAPTER 15

FANTASY

"We can't escape now....We are caught in a space-time that is impossible to break, unless we defeat them in their game...Our world and theirs can't exist at the same time... Only one will...and for that, we have to put ourselves before anything else in the world...We have to give our sweat and blood to save ourselves, the best way we can....To the best of our capacity...To let our spirit survive, even though it means destroying the other... They left us no other choice..... If we won't, it would be like wavering from a responsibility...How does your conscience let you live with it?" Skyra was saying to Henry, "We can't fight on their terms...But we can fake our death and outwit them....And then, when the world is cleaned of such elements, when we have proved their impotence, when they aren't strong any longer, exhausted and uprooted, we can return to our world, victorious with an immunity and a greater perspective, wearing a badge of victory....But before that, we have to wait...."

Chapter 16

REALITY

"Shut up, you stupid fool, shut up and listen to me...!!! From now on, you will act as I say...What you eat, drink, say and think, it will be decided by me, as and when I say... When I say sit you sit, and when I say stand you stand... Do you get it?? You know you are nothing without me... You don't have the courage worth two bits….Whatever you are, it's because of me, because I made you feel so.....Always made sure to keep you on pedestal high above....Don't act like you never knew....Or did you actually believe all that??... Now I want you to get this straight....No make-believe from now onwards....I want you to see me for what I actually am... What did you know about me, huh?.....", she said in a high-pitched tone, which sounded sarcastic.

Bault was struck like a lightning, wondering what he had done to exact such wrath. And the woman saying all this couldn't be his beloved wife.

"That girl who lives next-door is the root of all evil.....we are together in it now, it needed to be said...We were always...

But now, I want your whole-hearted participation...I want you to take an oath...You have been doing your bit, but that's not enough.....I don't want to give her an inch to spread... When she smiles, I can't sleep...When I see her moving, do you know how that makes me feel inside?....And by the way do you have any idea how unpredictably twisted she is turning out to be??....She is giving me the nightmares of a lifetime...!!! I hate every DNA in her body, every fibre of her being, every breath she takes...!! I want her 'soul' captured.... And you will help me achieve this...You have to be fully dedicated towards me.....It will work….It will trample her being...She will squirm with pain...And when she does that, only then you can expect me to be nice to you....The pressure is not enough for her now....You don't have the guts to scare me...You can't degrade a degraded person like me.... Earlier, I was just a part of your existence, but from now I am your whole existence....So you get it loud and clear that if my expectations from you aren't up to the mark, it's not I who is making you suffer...It's that devil out there..."

She paused to release a heave of air from her lungs. "This is not just my mission with you as a sidekick anymore...It is 'our mission' now...We are partners, and don't forget that when I win, which I am confident I will, the shine of the victory will not be just mine, but ours...Fifty-fifty...All you have to do is stick to my side...Let me be the master and follow my directions...And we will be the assured champions of the world....We will rise to an all-new morning...."

"You don't have any opinion in this....My say is your say...I want that sprouting shrub to be reduced to a stump....A damage beyond repair....Do you understand?", Ridaline snapped.

"I don't get this...What is.....Why is all this so important to you? Why can't we forget all this and live a normal life happily... As we were... You were so nice and then all of a sudden...", Bault finally blurted out.

"To understand that, you will need more lives than a cat and that too won't be enough for you...", she said.

He tried looking somewhere else, so he won't have to see her.

"You agree to the conditions mentioned above...?"

He shook his head enough to mean yes. He wanted the conversation to stop right there, it was making him feel sick.

"Whatever you do, remember this thing-you can't afford to hate me...", she said before letting him go.

Thus, the two minds intermingled, joined and collaborated to produce a hybrid species of two distinct minds, rather than two individual minds independent of each other. They were always aware of each other, of the common motive, of their partnership, of their involvement as in a secret society. They had their sleeves rolled and socks pulled up, arms loaded, guns pointed, sixth sense on high alert. Now, it was an open ground for battle, the animosity trebled, without any disguise. Bault had become equivalent to a medium, transferring the subconscious level between the two parties.

Skyra had chosen him as the new attacking zone, establishing a new second frontier- it was unmanageably tough for her. She also found that this strategy fired back-when she had felt content with her progress, she saw him making personal attempts to break the flow by surprising at times-he was turning out to be cleverer, as a result of the recently incorporated seeds–the devotion was faithful, it had turned him into a perfect pawn, himself unaware of the price of the fruits his efforts were bearing for Riddy. *It will all come back around*-Skyra said to herself, wishing he could hear her. But he was too blinded from the fog to even imagine that Skyra could turn it all around, make him pay the price, show the direness of his unwarranted headlong venture into the her life's personal domain. Frankly speaking, it was legible for him to play his part as he pleased, but the way he was messing things around, Skyra wanted to warn him not to play with fire. How much harmful it can prove to be, in the long run-that he would be screwed up, nonetheless. She did not know whether to pity him or sympathise with him, for having to bear the brunt on Riddy's behalf. Perhaps, he was not having any idea how much grit Skyra had. He thought Skyra's wickedness had a limit, and after that she was the same virtuous girl. All this told Skyra that she would have to raise her bar; if a person could be so awfully mind-washed, the only method left is to raise the bar. He had lost his insight on the whole affair, led by a single thrust of the band tied around his neck by Riddy.

Once, after a couple of days of her apparent absence from the warfront, they were away outside. Celebrating, Skyra knew. She knew it was the perfect time to execute her attack-very casually and coldly. She waited, checking up again and again, drawing her curtains and spying through the window. It felt lowering and restless, but she knew the result will outscore the effort. She was roaming in the balcony, having a hard time holding the volcano inside her from erupting before time. Leaning across on the railing she saw the Cadillac swerve into the driveway. Those 30 seconds were the most relaxing duration of her life, more than she had ever experienced in the chambers of a spa. It looked so natural, but the flair of her manners conveyed it clearly that it was planned and she was known to the pangs of irrevocable loathing that would follow later in the next door.

Thus she had turned them into a basic need of her life. She had made herself learn the art of manoeuvring events so they would know how one's own existence can feel a curse because it was a source of 'guilty pleasures' to one's enemies, whatsoever the reason be-ignorance, underestimation or simply a mistake. Whatever, Riddy would have enough time to nag and censure about it, privately, without anybody or anyway to her avail; to retrospect how Skyra had outwitted her yet again; that a loophole was still present and she were too smart to pry through it to freedom. She couldn't bear the fact how Skyra stood there, flaunting her success. She just won't bite the bait, all of Ridaline's attempts were going in vain, she speculated seriously how more sharp Skyra would prove to be. The hue and cry clamoured internally to manifest in the daily routine.

Skyra had decided to change her apartment within Primrose residential complex itself. She wanted to start afresh; she realised the lack of distance was too much. It felt as if the Krummers resided with her, and shared her apartment with them. But before that she would have to turn the conditions feasible. It had to come as a surprise, when least expected, at the wrong time to leave them marooned. She knew how badly they needed her. The last few straws needed to be picked out and then she would be free.

There were times when Skyra knew Riddy was fully-geared and eager to display her power by testing on her. Those days, Skyra would remain home-bound to ignore any such encounter. This too, was a mechanism Skyra had bartered from her. The restlessness would be too much; so Riddy would step out and experiment her effect on the strangers she met on the street. Satisfied, she would return and keep her energy in store. Skyra reflected what kind of a life they had turned theirs into, living life vicariously this way. What would happen if all this habituated psyche were to come to an end? Maybe then, they would realise their idiosyncrasy and get their shock, that how much they had diverged from normalcy, and how addicted they were to her presence, which was the sole bridge of connection between the two. Life had been so bland before, not colourful as now. Skyra could see her through their high hat behaviour, that it was them that were the needy ones for association. She would use it as a tool of irony to smack it on their faces, and then there would be a happily ever-after. There would be no spectator on whom to impose their melodrama.

Among the series of encounters that followed, Riddy would come prepared after her experimentation on neighbours and the like, but would be sullen and baffled equally on seeing that Skyra had built her impenetrable exterior, a safety halo encircling her. The Krummer couple kept themselves updated in private, and there was a gooey paste sticking between them. They felt glad to be alive on earth, to feel that their lives had a purpose and that they were doing a good job as a team, surging through and tackling the most heinous threat to the world. They wanted respect and superiority and if it won't be granted, they would move mountains to turn the picture 360 degrees around. Skyra could never imagine her comparison to Ridaline- it would be an inimitable insult to her. However difficult they could make life for her, distort the reality to whatever extent, but she won't let up-there was always the option of not relenting and fighting-there was always a way, even though it would not be easy.

Come hell or high water, she would not concede-this precisely was who she was; this was her identity. In normal circumstances, everybody appears to be the same, but it's these eccentric situations that differentiate people from each other. They had made the circumstances such that no human value was attached to her that she might even be considered an entity, let alone of a dignified woman of substance. She was dethroned from her pinnacle, and she accepted that. She could not act oblivious to a fact if she saw it vividly; it was ground-breaking initially to see such gruesome occurrences, but she accepted it all and fought from whatever ground she stood on. But deep down, nobody could touch her concept of self-image, it was intact and unscratched. This feigning of all falsities, false self-esteem would just be a temporary fad; it wouldn't hold out against the sharp contrast of truth. Her strength wasn't so trivial, as they thought.

Sometimes Skyra asked herself, why had she undertaken such a task, why was it necessary? But she realised it was too late, she had made the decision long ago- there comes a time when one's inaction harms oneself, how much can one pretend to not see? It was her task, only she had the capability; it had happened after their lives had crossed paths, so automatically the burden fell on her. It was not just a threat to her, but on her pretext, the whole mankind was in danger. One can forget and move on, but only to a limit. When barriers such as these are crossed, inaction is like hitting the plough on one's own feet. They had made her the point of ridicule, so it held a personal significance to her, just like it did to Riddy. Now her sole aim rested on the point of snatching away their peace, which directly came from destroying Riddy. So much for hatred...She knew she could never in any way explain this to any person on earth...Her perception won't be bought by others...She had realised her innocence had turned into an albatross around her neck...She did not want to fit into the 'civilised' group anymore....She had cultivated her alter-ego well...It worked, although Riddy did not show any sign of letting up, rather fielded the attacks well and responded back well to her level best...At times, trying to scare her away by her piercing gaze and raising her voice....

Once when she thought she would be alone, she was caught unawares by Riddy sitting in the balcony, a curled-up creature, showing her obstinate defiance like a stiff stone..... She trembled and came back....It was not the person, but the noxious fumes it carried.......Revolving the whole picture upside down....That how fantastic the view was from that side...She wanted to yell that Riddy was not battling her.... but she was fighting the reality....Riddy wanted to overcome reality by testing the force of her non-reality on her...That Riddy's non-reality would be a living testimony by an assured experimentation on Skyra....It would get that certificate of distinction and a licence to be a guaranteed success because it worked on her nemesis, the most virtuous goddess. Skyra knew what she represented and that Riddy's implausible vision would be far from reach....She might reach too close, but the uncoverable gap would always remain.........

She would feel that two criminals were at large, from whom the world would catch the disease and spread to others....That they had to be stopped to save the world.... That how hopelessly lost they were, busy constructing a formula they believed to be done with her...How mind-numbingly stupid and horrific at the same time...Their contempt towards Skyra had grown to ridiculous levels... Skyra would telepathically swing to and fro from the alternate world.....She had sworn to wash away their plans. It would be stupid if Riddy thought that she could, on the basis of her superlative abilty, however meticulous they were, take away Skyra's self-esteem; the position she enjoyed for the time being might be the one that actually Skyra deserved and belonged, but it won't hold for long. Skyra had applied the theory of relativity in form; if they thought they were the only ones pulling at one end of the tug and Skyra would just watch the show of her own downfall, they were highly mistaken. They would have to foray against her resistance; it was down to the wire.

Bault was now used to living in a state of constant fear, though he would not commit the mistake of stating it in such clear terms. He would have preferred to think of it a transient phase, which after sometime would make the way for a prosperous undisputed future as a result of their back-breaking efforts. All he had to do was hold on. He had clearly understood how obnoxiously harmful the girl was; he stayed wary of her even while sleeping. She needed to be damned if she was giving Riddy such a hard time. Why could she not keep silent and put her feet down to Riddy? Everything seemed to be synchronous and perfect, but for the whims of that girl-the bad apple. Afterall, Ridaline was a well-learned intellectual civilised woman par excellence, whose ideal picture went without saying. Nobody he knew could dominate her in conversation; he himself was at a loss to escape her eagle eyes, she knew everything just by looking at him, even the things he wanted to hide. Moreover, her control was immaculate; he was happy to be on the stronger side, safe and above the rest. It was his duty to obey her demands, as required of a faithful husband. He felt happy and satisfied when she took utmost care of him and suffused the surroundings with an excited vitality, boosting his ego-if his efforts could bring such gifts to him, he was more than obliged to agree with her. On a second thought, that was the only method to keep his relationship going strong, albeit it was based on an ultimatum.

Ridaline had started to find matchless ecstasy in pitting her tensile strength against Skyra's. She marvelled at her own skill at the way she had made Skyra to represent the cause of all miseries and failures of Bault's life, an obstacle that needed to be looked down worse than a garbage bin. She had encouraged him to take all his infuriation out on her, when she knew that it was she herself who put him through hell to make her ends meet. She knew that the way she was treating Bault, she would change the entire wiring of his brain, its structure and function, for the rest of his life-it would change the nature of the relation they had. But, it was indispensable at this point and worth it in the days to come. She had without his conscious consent, put him at stake. It was a tough decision but a safe bet. If it could bring her the achievement of her mission, then she might as well humour herself. Now when she thought of Skyra, which was most of the time, she did not feel the usual stab of jealousy, but a feeling of malicious pleasure. She had never fully realised her own dangerous combination with him, his dutiful obedience under her masterminded leadership was perfect to give Skyra the worst days of her life. She liked to think of her writhing in pain in the loneliness of her room, that it hurt her and contorted her face and left her speechless-to see all this even when she didn't wish to see and couldn't change it either.

As days passed the dichotomy between Skyra's two personalities became greater in magnitude. She had developed the ability to telepathically fluctuate to and fro from her reality to the Riddy's fantasyland, like a swinging pendulum. She was curious to see the future consequences, that what would be left of Riddy's world if Skyra suddenly disappeared forever. Added to that, with the last word. She would be free forever of the sticky sycophants, and would not have to force herself to think about them when she didn't want to. There would be no necessity to solve her anymore, the spaces in her head would be evacuated. The battle would be called on hold, all of a sudden with no definite results. But the most satisfying fact would be that it would be she to call the shots. She would never lose the feel of the depressing days she had seen (that she had never believed possible till now); that one person single-handedly could turn her life into a living hell; added to that that nobody was there to put an end to it. Ironically, only aiding it the best way possible. This was a fact she considered more horrific than Halloween or getting shot directly-because that would be instant, but this was slow and steady, and it killed the person while still alive, and many at a time, and could spread rapid and fast like tuberculosis. She brooded, misty-eyed, at how the pillars of her existence were plundered one by one and she could do nothing because there didn't exist a law for such crime.

Seldom would someone have undertaken such a challenge as Riddy did- trying to destroy every trace of reality. She had been considerably successful, they were geared to go a long way; and the deeper she was going into it, the riskier she was making it for herself, unknowingly. Because, Skyra thought, the farther they go, the more shameful it would be and more difficult to come back. Higher the fall, greater the injuries. More so, if no turning point was possible. Height of evil, would also be the height of stupidity, if proved ineffective. It could render life tasteless, if their biggest dream was turned to an utter failure. Skyra wondered if the amount of hatred for her was so much now, when she hadn't even played half of her cards, then how more can they hate if she played till the end, when they would realise how clearly she understood everything from the beginning. All they could do was clean plain hate in the confines of their room, toss their fists in the air like they made her do. Riddy had a great expertise in seeding problem in mind, and was taking utmost care to leave no leeway for betterment of mind; in fact, Skyra was well aware how badly she hoped that Skyra stopped functioning for life.

But Skyra was well aware of the effects of her secret move. She waited for the perfect timing. Lately, she had been enforcing many an encounter with them to dare them for more duels. But, through their veil of enforced self-value, they would show no such inclination, rather would show conceited indifference. She did it to make sure they did not complain later for insufficiencies. She knew that the guidance lay with her; if she vanished, they would be shocked, groping for a hold, to know where to take it from there. So Skyra kept the excitement afloat, to keep them bracing themselves from a disaster to happen, which never came except in small spouts. In the interactions, Skyra made sure all her issues were resolved, and shown that she could stand through all threats they held and that they had nothing that could possibly make her afraid. Riddy felt all this to be strange, so passed the torch into Bault's hands and pushed him to the fore. It could not end this way, she knew; she had put herself on hold, storing all the energy, waiting to chase the next opportunity by catching the hint in Skyra's movements. In that brief moment of halt, came the perfect timing to strike the rod. Skyra chose a time so that the zone was clear of any sort of attack.

As she unpacked her things in her new apartment, she was faintly aware that they were thunderstruck. But all she knew was that how excruciatingly long she had to stretch her mind for one moment, putting all actions at a hold, and now she could put herself at ease, let all the strain unwind. Three days later, when she came to pick up her remaining paraphernalia, she deliberately slammed the door hard- first, to release the suppression of the previous days, and secondly to denote the sealing of the saga.

Chapter 17

FANTASY

"This is what they mean when they say: The world would be a better place...", she said, prancing around the lush green spread of the mountainous slope. The grass seemed to collect the sparking luminescence from the sun and the blend of the hue thus produced glistened brilliantly.

He clasped her hand and turned to face her upfront. With a soft caress of his hand, he drew the strands of her hair aside, then held her face in the cup of his hands.

"Are you free now...?", he asked.

She winked her eyes delicately.

"I love you....", he said.

Then they kissed gently.

"You look peacefully serene today", Aunt said.

"It's a new beginning", was all she said.

Chapter 18

REALITY

The wall between her and the world had been devastated. It was heaven on earth. All she could feel around her was the calm. She went around for walks, drinking in the freshness of a new chapter of her life. She saw people with a new outlook, which she hadn't seen in years- they appeared feathery light, and not disturbing to the vision. She let the tranquillity resonate with the vibrations of her heart, mind and brain simultaneously. She felt an inner peace brimming inside. She felt no need to think about Ridaline; neither did she pop up in her mind. People looked different and harmless- she felt happy to think that the Krummers were left with their dramatic world to themselves. Here, she would live alone without a demon on the prowl to devour her.

She thought of herself as a butterfly which they wanted to catch, she flitted from tree to tree, they chased her and now they had reached a stage where they found themselves stranded in a jungle, not knowing the way out. She had had the last word and she chortled when she imagined how angrily stupefied Riddy would be. That's all she thought, nothing else. In Mrs. and Mr. Krummer's eyes, she was the fugitive, on the run after perpetrating a punishable offence; because she had taken away their platform to exhibit their power-packed stunts on her-the only means of satisfaction in this vast yet empty world; she was the only person in the world on whom their methods had to work, to give instant gratifying results. Domination of her meant domination of the world. She knew how fortunate they considered themselves that she had to be their neighbour, that their paths crossed this way; it was like hitting a goldmine. Skyra exulted in the feeling that she had averted the end of the world; and won't be haunted by Ridaline anymore. That a life existed beyond her and she was living it right now.

She could not describe how insanely happy she was to reopen her senses to the better aspect of the world; it was time to switch off the part of the brain that had been activated. She felt that she had missed on something in life; and that she had covered the length of 8 months in one go, only from one point to another, even though there had been many points in between. Instead of taking the road, rock-climbing to the summit. But, looking at the spacious walls around her, she knew that she had achieved something in return and it would remain with her forever; till the last day of her life, it would show in every act she would take. The journey was arduous, if truth be told. She nailed it, somehow with the single device of her acumen. It would be impact-making on the generations to come. She had been living on an edge and she detested it immensely. But she was in the Goldie Sachs zone now, thriving with profuse space around her. Their world must have collapsed like a house of cards. She had thrown the paradox of their scheme in their faces.

It was ceasefire. It was like homecoming; resuming her normal channels of thought. Her days in exile were over. She fell, but most importantly she rose. All she wanted was to be herself, pick up the pieces of her life and thread them together again. The gases bottled up inside her exploded to be occupied by clean air of the new surroundings. There was no need to constantly fake, mask oneself, to be on the alert, to be trampled spiritually.

An essential merit or demerit of all the past days was that her imaginative power had grown massively. Ostensibly enough, she had made her truce with them. They had to accept that their projections did not ring true; that theoretical result was different from application. It was the penalty they paid for sending her to the gallows. They had robbed her of her honour, now they were on a tailspin. Now, both her personalities were at one with each other. The bugs eating her from inside were shaken off. She wondered which direction they would herald now. Their wrongdoings had given her life a rust and it could never be salvaged any way. It had shaped her for life. So she had taken away the only thing Riddy wanted so awfully voraciously- the subconscious superiority- in absence. Skyra had made her understand the notion that one should never cross the formidable lines. Cynically, the only method available to them to escape the uncomfortable position was to cross the line to another level. But it wasn't possible given the conditions; Skyra had made use of a secret trump card-distance.

Skyra loved to spend time in her new abode, when she roamed around, she saw specific outlines and definite shapes, not obscure or blurred lines. She could not contain herself anymore; a halo of charged ecstasy hovered over her head. She knew, in the deepest nook and crannies of her mind, that the foundation of their 'castle in the air' was not holding up, to carry the weight; and they needed her guidance to strengthen it. It filled her with delight. Once, she was passing by the street of her old apartment and her mind aligned with the centre of her gravity, as though she suddenly got aware that she were standing in a spotlight.

Back at the fashion house, she found a quiet satisfaction in simply observing people and fitting small remarks wherever necessary. She felt secure in their company, because each one of them was not Ridaline; she knew what Riddy was and it was comforting to be around people who were not as lethal as she. She was the life of shows all over again. The separation of her bond with Riddy held a sarcasm that was beyond any measure that any personal act could convey. It meant Riddy wrestling with a constant yet intangible presence of Skyra-invincible because it offered no pitch to drop the ball, however strong contender one was. It was left trailing in the air; it was Skyra's answer to them for the same ghastly torture that she had been through. She was even, although she was aware it would take some time to straighten the tilted balance. It was two weeks later, when she woke up to behold the grand beginning which the day signified that day onwards. It was evident; every speck screamed that she had vanquished Riddy in her game. She watched television, the programmes were soothing like a balm. She had played her cards close to her chest and it had paid off, if it felt like this. When one openly declared villainous disagreement, there was no guilt involved. She was doubtful about the amount of anguish that accompanied in A-86 of Primrose residential complex.

Back in their quarter, the Krummers felt like they had been played for a fool. They had lost their lustre, being with people wasn't as fulfilling anymore. They were now keenly aware of their presence as definite people, and not simply as dolls of muscle and bone to be played with, as they wished. To make matters worse, they had lost their control; the guests had become overbearing and they were completely at a loss to know which way to steer across. It was difficult to keep their head above water, they had never known that their re-joining with the world minus the model would come to this. They realised that their perception needed to be improved, their point of view had been messed up by her. The projections had fallen short, their own methods were failing and they did not have any plan to go ahead.

It was a clean sweep by the girl, and a standstill for them. Except...except if they saw her again....then they would know exactly what to do....It was tough like this, hitting a rough patch....It was a do or die situation. Riddy had known by the intensity of the bang of the door how much more energy was needed to be extracted to raise the game to the required stage. She had thrown the sympathy-deriving fit again, made Skyra sound the reason for all their miseries, inflated Bault up to the highest level, had drilled it deep inside that now it was all up to him to save their prestige from tatters, and that his too resided with her, because they were together in it and that all the support in the world was with him from her side. She also made clear that if he succeeded, it would be the last stumbling block in their mission and the way to a permanent happiness would be paved forever. Bault was the board for climbing-he had agreed to it long ago; he had even performed once with her, but this time, he had to handle it all alone. Both geared up for the next milestone to be set. It would be a hit and trial method, they kept their fingers crossed. It was at 11:05 am, when Bault returned from depositing the laundry, that Riddy knew by the joviality of his appearance that the impossible was achieved.

CHAPTER 19

FANTASY

The atmosphere of Helfung had darkened even more, with Ridaline acting on her peak level. She demanded greater devotion from her people; they relegated themselves for her sake. No individual mind was permitted; everybody was a part of the great social soup. Seeds of equality and sharing were sown, having personal thoughts was a blasphemy. "Happiness is a guilt", such ideas were ingrained deep and anybody opposing it was made a pariah. The weak were immediately engulfed and those courageous enough to question found themselves bowing against the crumbling pressure. People were taught to find pride in their ineptitude and to look down at any high-spirited person. Soon the movement had a huge mass sweeping into its direction. Every nook and cranny was toxified.

Sitting on the floor of the prison, Skyra saw the surroundings around her. It brought back the memory of the first time when she had discovered herself in this place- and now she was back again. Somehow, both the events were similar. Only this time, she felt that the inertia inside were dissolved, as though she were weightless. She was bewildered to grasp the essence of her existence; that one could feel and not feel at the same time, that one existed and did not exist simultaneously, like water vapour, one whose presence can't be denied nor be acknowledged. It was a surreal feeling and she hated it. She hated having to feel it, to have lived to witness it; it was worse than being dead, because death allowed one to escape it. She was done for, she felt. She recalled Henry..................

CHAPTER 20

REALITY

The shock had taken 3 days to set. Initially, there was denial. It rose to anger and hatred, and all the feelings that she had buried inside resurfaced again. When she fully grasped the gist of the scenario, standing at the edge of the membrane that demarcated her reality and their fantasy-she broke. It meant losing it all, starting a brand new lap all over again, and most of all conjuring up her other-self again, which had started taking form already. It also meant, she had more layers to penetrate. Riddy had incomprehensibly created a denser intricacy. After such a long-drawn struggle, Skyra had finally found long-sought peace and happiness, only to lose it all over again. Again, all of it went to their store. And pretty shamelessly on their part; like a coward, attacking from behind when it was time-out, when the decision had been made and the warfield emptied.

But his presence showed that he was extending the game, and he was ready to cut down of a chunk of his false esteem if it was needed, as his act conveyed. But the fact was that even though she would survive, she won't be able to expand her level unless opportunities cropped up to have direct contact with Riddy. The equations inferred that she was to be the only receptor, that too, by surprise, unexpectedly- just like the stunt Bault pulled on. Eye for an eye. By his chameleon-like cautious pounce from behind, it was clear that he knew beforehand of the results that he was trying to be materialised. By a little trimming of his haughtiness, which was completely unanticipated, he had turned the equations in his favour. To speak the truth, it was not his presence that was devastating, but the gases of non-reality that emanated from him, which clashed sharply to destroy Skyra's sense of being and left her in a state of jiffy, with himself flying to a safe escape as quickly as possible, not knowing where he was going, the car controlling him instead of the other way round. But it was not Bault that Skyra hated, he had only planted the block; it was Riddy, the woman behind him who had won using him so deftly. It was like they had snatched away her tool and used it to their advantage, so easily and made a parody of it before her, and she was the laughingstock now. Now she was left alone in the balcony, for her turn of reply, if she ever had the chance to. A dead barren stretch of desert lay before her; she had to start it again from a scratch. It was all summated to be reduced to a zero. She had believed that she was the one having the upper hand, but Riddy, by her sheer determination and calculative mind, had once again toppled her.

The Krummers had crossed the line yet again, for the third time. Skyra wanted to take it to a level so that their eyes would be opened far-wide, but it would mean sinking into the small form again. He had absorbed the fruits of her hard work and carried it to his master to enjoy them. Time would be needed to prove, probably another year. She was back to hell. Her enemies won't let her live in peace, they hadn't yet forgotten or let go of her. She was back to the negligible state, she deactivated her Facebook account. Did they know what was at the end of the flight? It wouldn't be everlasting, for eternity...Only as long as their souls would hold out to pool all the energy they have. She could not live like this, but she had taken the hint he had dropped, that they were going far. They had short-circuited the world, and were celebrating yet again. She felt like a deflated can again; the echo of the upcoming days was bad. It was depression, with hardships as the icing. She made a decision-she will not rest, until she was done with them. All other sorts of progress had to be stopped, unless it was directly concerned with them. It would be a hiatus, but not for no reason.

The tension was like the folds in her brain were pulled apart and straightened out. It was like countering the united strength breaking down on her- as if the weight of the world was on her back, the future of every individual had altered, and it was better than hers. She knew that this, precisely was the maximum and they can't go any further. And the only way she could be avenged now was if the game came to a full circle. Halfway was one point too behind, just an anti-climax; the end-point would be the climax. And for that, she would have to wait, she didn't know how long, or whether the last will shape up to be reached ever. All she knew that she had to do her bit and the rest would have to follow naturally. Nothing could be more fool-proof than a game well-planned enough to look as if the choices that they made themselves was their pathway to doom. In other words, that the girl they set out to destroy isn't the same girl anymore, this and only this could lead to the debacle; when their principles won't apply similar to the deduced results. That whatever they assumed was not actual, but merely hypothetical. Skyra did not name it revenge; it felt too cheap and inappropriate. It was simply breaking free from the chains, and coaxing them to fall in their own gambit.

Riddy was well aware that Skyra was trapped, that the final block hampering transfer from non-reality to reality had been put. She moved around basking in the new and the finally-found delight of victory. It was unbelievable that her laborious and consistent mind-work had paid off. The final tiny straw that had been hanging nastily over her eyes had been removed. The wait was over. But the victory was so huge that she gave herself one-month's time to swallow it completely, so that at the end of the time she knew exactly the massiveness of the ultimate triumph known to humans; sizing down the difference between what position she stood and where that girl. She jumped in excitement when she realised that the difference was incredibly huge. She had finally succeeded in ousting her forever and the throne now belonged to her. Her eyes twinkled whenever she used to think of what inferno she must be going through. She hoped she could see her in pain, but she contented herself by imagining her lying in some floor, destroyed and devastated, paying the penances for her attempt to meddle with Riddy, knowing that how actually weak she was against Riddy's mettle. But she found it better to think that she was smouldering with fury and wanted to smash her head right off the top.

"*It's not yet over..........*", Skyra kept saying to herself.

Chapter 21

FANTASY

She felt like being hurled back to the beginning of time, when reality and logic started to hold meaning and all it needed was a big explosion to throw it in order. She felt that at that point, all the moments she had seen in life ever since had been erased out, summated to an absolute zero. And that whatever she was going to do from now, whatever step she would take would be against all tolerance known to man; even elastic when stretched has a breaking point, but she would not allow herself to break. Hanging by a thread, she would continue if that was the requirement of her tough destiny. When one lost the wings, one had to crawl and that's what she would do.

She did not hate Countess Ridaline, they were not just enemies, it was not just a battle; when it is important one could give it these names, but when the importance transcended to unsurpassed levels, beyond the boundary of every comprehensible concept, calling it important becomes just an understatement. It acquires an enormous proportion to spread out and merge with the essence of every movement, act and sound; it becomes the very state of things, the true being of situations, the ultimate kaleidoscope of time. She was all set to suspend her senses, to destroy all her ego. All she had was the gift of the ostentatious end of time, a false stop, of which she had the power to set again in a new direction. She had one more chance; she was the needle in a compass and she could set any direction she liked. The only trouble being that there was less than a nanometre to inch through. They said that even time was not absolute, it had flaws like matter, she would find yet another crack. The game was not over, it appeared like it had just begun. A new phase, marked by Skyra's rebirth.

Now the only way left to shake herself free of the gigantic burden on her head was to demolish the prison. Only then, she would be avenged and she knew too well that she had the capacity, and the ability, that it started all because of her and it would end because of her too. She would go one step too far of the maximum, but would not relent. She vowed to make them pay for the damage, and to impose penalty for the innumerable days of pain and wait and incompleteness, for living with a bleeding wound that healed only to be mauled again.

All doors were closed, all her ways had been proven to fall short and she was engulfed in a dense and vicious psychological cocoon. The odds were clearly against her, but she had to try at least. Otherwise, how would she know? So that, years later when she would come across unanswered questions, she would tell herself that she did all she could.

She did not need an answer anymore, she just had to try. The answers had taken a backseat, they would come of their own accord, if they ever will. The prison was her target now, she had all the clues and she would see if it held against her might. That was all she wanted, just that. The result was unknown and unseen, a mystery and it would unravel itself with time. Her enemies would be wary of it and avoid it strongly, and even succeed to a degree, but she would go beyond that point and beyond that and beyond that and further till the pressure made them twist and turn. She would lay down the rule and they had to conform correspondingly because now they had no excuse in universe to find a way out. There was no way back to reality, to her world, to Prestoria. She would turn herself to embrace the prison for now- until she destroys it. She would turn the albatross around her neck into a necklace.

Chapter 22

REALITY

She felt a massive block between her and every other person, tough and thick like a mountain rock, deflecting any flow of emotion back on its way. She was standing at the event horizon, at the edge of reality and non-reality, hanging just at the right place eccentrically, and even a hair's breadth of staggering balance could send her spiralling into a series of unpleasant events, unredeemed forever. This was what meant to be left in limbo; she had lost the humour of the irony that her method had been used on her; her enemies had successfully turned the tables on her again. She felt disoriented and reduced to a heap by that giant tornado. All the risks she had taken, all the drastic transformations she had plastered on herself were for nothing, only for her to see this day. She had respectfully bowed out, citing a free road. But even that wasn't enough; she had been dragged back to it. The sarcasm and the mortification was unbearable. She found herself wanting to kill and thankful.

It was when she had gone to buy groceries in the evening from the local store at Votrade Street, when Skyra's eyes set on fresh flowers being sold nearby. She picked three magenta daisies and rummaged through her purse to grab some money. After paying the florist, as she started to leave, she retreated a few steps back. Her eyes caught sight of Brickbee's, in the front window of which was taped a big sticker. She climbed 2 steps at the entrance to have a closer look. It had written on it:

"Sculpture Show Tonight At 7:30 pm by Ridaline Krummer. Tickets available at counter"

A rush of adrenaline shot up in her stomach to give goosebumps on her skin. Was it luck or a cosmic force? She walked up to the counter and bought a ticket, her manners like those of a trained con-man.

At 7:45 pm exact, she changed her dress and spruced herself up in front of the mirror. Her hands were shaking. She could see nothing in the mirror; except her very own purpose. She was acting like a customised robot ordained to perform a task. The minutes felt anxious, like an assassin getting equipped with his weapons.

Quickly slinking to the street's cold air, she turned a block and reached Brickbee's. She paused for a second and took a deep breath. *It is important*, she told herself. Then she stepped inside. The crowd present was neither large nor small; there were one or two guests coming slowly. She surveyed the hall; she was not interested in the sculptures. She pretended to appreciate them. Gradually, she moved to the centre of the hall; her eyes scouring the place. Then the time came.

Ridaline was surrounded by two men and two women, having a tête-à-tête out of earshot. Then the humdrum conversation stopped for a moment.

"*Forgive me Ridaline, but you asked for it*", Skyra mumbled. She stood singled out from the crowd so that she could be spotted easily. Her eyes were transfixed on Riddy. "*Look at me Riddy, look at me…*"

After 10 seconds, Riddy's line of eyesight aligned with that of Skyra. But Ridaline had not recognised her yet. A profuse smile, sarcastic and mischievous, spread on Skyra's lips. Ends of Ridaline's lips had started to turn up a little. Then she figured out the familiar face. It was not a smile, it was scorn, calling out to challenge. Ridaline's face got drained of colour, but Skyra continued to smile. Riddy looked as if she was inside an airplane approaching a crash. Her face betrayed everything that the surprise carried- that she didn't expect her here, and that too in this demeanour. Then seriousness of the indignation reflected in her face- like a supernova explosion. The anger was palpable- and it didn't allow Skyra to smirk anymore. Skyra turned and left, the load off her chest. She was evenly redeemed and it was priceless. She was glad she met Ridaline in life.

CHAPTER 23

FANTASY

It felt like an earthquake. Then there was a rumbling sound that resonated throughout the prison domain.

Skyra, sitting with her knees propped up, was startled. She lifted herself and walked towards the chamber entrance which was bounded by prison bars. Another sound followed. Then another. From the distance, she could make out a stone plummeting down from the inside of hall. Then, a stone belonging to the corner of the roof of her chamber dropped down. The impact shook the floor vehemently. It was as if gravity had won and the structural components had given away. The clamour was reverberating all around and the building blocks kept flinging down.

Half of the roof had vanished into thin air rendering the chamber open to the skies. The blocks were falling here and there. Skyra dodged herself left and right. A block came smashing down on her head, but to her amazement, it didn't hurt. The floor went crashing down, taking Skyra along with it. Within 3 seconds, the whole structure crumbled to pieces. Waving away the dust with her hands, Skyra rose up from the pile of debris. She was free now.

She had to look for Henry. When she found him, he seemed pleasantly surprised. They hugged each other and kissed wildly, erasing out the sadness that the moments of separation had built up. They made love till early morning.

Chapter 24

REALITY

Skyra was immersed in euphoria as the 'happy' chemicals in her brain shot up in the days that followed. Her encounter with Ridaline on the day of the exhibition was recorded in her mind, and it was replayed again and again. Never before in her life had she had so much to gloat about. Basking in glory, she felt herself protected and Ridaline defeated. It was obvious in all things, in the food she prepared, the programmes she watched or the streets she sauntered.

Her subconscious bonding with the Krummers was stronger than ever; the sarcasm greater. The connection had crept into the innermost recesses of her mind; she was aware that Riddy was conscious about her all the time, just as she was about her. Now there was no denying about the game, and all three were part of it. It was perhaps the most important thing in the world.

She returned to the rampwalks as a reborn-dead-reborn person. Like new sprouts shooting up in a seed; her batteries recharged, life had returned back to her. She didn't care who the "Fashion Futurista" crown went to; all she knew was the storm in her mind had settled down to tranquillity. It was over. But what she didn't know that she was safe only as long as she didn't see them, which won't be for long.

"I need my revenge, Bault…Our revenge….", Ridaline was saying, "Won't you get it for us…?", she sobbed.

2 MONTHS LATER

Skyra had made it a rule not be present in the balcony more than five seconds. She had disciplined herself to it. Even that much was a risk, but it was minimal. In the 5 seconds which she had given herself as a lease on life, she had no idea that danger was lurking. Bault came, his car like a flying comet, tearing along the street, planting a full-stop to anything that came in between.

It would be an understatement to say that Skyra hated his guts. The chemicals in her brain dried up; the radiance gone. She had to find a permanent remedy. Enough of all this, she thought. First I will do away with them, then rejoin the world. Enough of healing and getting hurt again. I want all the hurt in one blow, not in catches. For once and for all.

Chapter 25

FANTASY

"It is hereby declared that the kingdom of Prestoria is henceforth dissolved and annexed by the country of Helfung. All ruling powers now reside with her majesty, the Countess of Helfung". The announcement was made at Hauris Point, at the colosseum and throughout the country.

'Devoid of any desire'- These were the only four words needed to describe Skyra, as she turned to be. For the first time, she didn't know what to do. Her Prestoria was gone. Her life was shattered and nothing was left. She could do nothing about it.

But now was also the time to rise. What answers would she give her father?

CHAPTER 26

REALITY

Bault had not shown up for a fortnight, which explained it had ended the right way for him and Ridaline. It also elucidated that it was them who had had the last laugh, hands down.

The wall clock was ticking. Skyra stepped outside. She strolled around the streets, feeling nothing. Suddenly, she felt a strong urge to go to Shopping Centre of Primrose complex. She had a gut feeling where the Krummers might be. She had to check.

It was inevitable. She saw them standing near a magazine store, talking with a man who appeared to be a friend. Skyra made her presence again. She walked, very confidently towards the store and picked up a copy of "Starstruck". She spoke, loudly enough for the couple to hear, "How much is this??"

For a second, Skyra was terrified that the store-owner won't answer. But he did.

"That's six euros", he said humbly.

"Oh!! Six euros!!!", Skyra screeched, at the top of her voice.

The store-owner looked disoriented.

"And……This one??", she asked, swaying another magazine into her hands.

"Seven euros, ma'm", came the reply.

"Whoa!! Seven euros!!!," Skyra said excitedly, acting like a surprised little kindergarten girl.

She was aware of the trio's sound waves reaching her eardrums, but she won't acknowledge them. All noise filtered off to leave the voice of a single person- Ridaline's. Within milliseconds, Riddy had decided to make the most of situation, to use the opportunity to her advantage. She increased her pitch to greater than usual.

The scene appeared to be having two systems containing different people in each, oblivious of the other's presence. The only thing Skyra was aware of was Riddy's voice which kept fluctuating in between Skyra's. Skyra could not refrain from turning an angle to catch Riddy's glance. Riddy won't react, Skyra couldn't tell if she was shocked or not. But then, Ridaline was unlike any other woman- she could absorb any shock better than many. Skyra continued her conversation with the store-owner. She felt she had dramatized the scene properly; she had incorporated Ridaline's element perfectly and mimicked her correctly. Then, there was a big pause. Skyra knew that a pair of eyeballs was surveying her. She bought a copy of 'Sweet Nothings', and went away.

Chapter 27

FANTASY

The dethroned Queen formed an army to rebel against the new government. It was both easy and hard. Not all co-operated. Some were like Henry, their own country annexed and forced to live in Helfung, despite not wanting to; and the brainwashed ones needed to be stripped of the blindfold over their eyes.

Her soldiers marched throughout the country, crossing swords with the army of Helfung.

CHAPTER 28

REALITY

Skyra wanted to break all barriers, to take everything to the maximum level- only then, things could shape up. She also wanted her enemies to know her for who she actually was, rather than what they presumed her to be.

She spotted the car, parked on the street. Skyra's heart started to beat faster. She waited in anticipation. She didn't know which shop they were in, so she started dilly-dallying.

The trio faced each other again. This time, on the pavement. Bault increased his speed as soon as he saw her, so he was ten steps ahead of Ridaline. His confidence was like that of a gladiator wearing a bullet-proof jacket. Skyra avoided eye-contact with him. She had come for Ridaline, he was just a sidekick. Smiling, she looked up to face Riddy and saw two small contemptful eyes, convicting her of inhumane deeds. Skyra's eyes fired back with fury. Flustered, Riddy's footsteps got swifter for a second. But only for a second.

Chapter 29

FANTASY

"Our 256 men have died", said Bault, concerned. "Do you think it's wise to......"

Ridaline cut him in between, "Stop it, Bault...How many times I have told you?? We have to win...We will..... Look around you..This castle, with you and me as the rulers.....Don't you like it? Don't you want it forever?"

"I do....", he said, "But we are losing."

"Don't worry...People are with us....Do you think a handful of such as 125 men can fight an army of 1000...?"

"But she has escaped every time....And this time, she is openly fighting..."

"That little ninja is up for grabs....Let her do what she wants...The prey is walking towards the predator....How simple can that be??"

"I feel we are not safe....", he said, casting forth his fears.

"Don't forget you are with me...I have never been vanquished, neither will ever be...Just make sure you are on my side, darling...."

Chapter 30

REALITY

Skyra kept going to the Shopping Centre everyday, in hopes of having an encounter with the Krummers. She was desperate for it, because only that would give her a new direction. It would provide her with a doorway to enter their world, and thus a solution to the whole affair. She was well aware that she was risking her whole self-esteem at this stage. *It will pay off in the end*, she said to herself. The best way to lose a fear is to challenge it. And she was ready to go to any length for that.

They had taken away her peace of mind; they had not complied when the war had been called off by her. Now, it was her turn to retort back and keep them on their toes. Things had reached such a level when nothing could be planned anymore. It was also a point of no return.

From this moment on, for Skyra it was a 'do-or-die' situation all the time. At times, Skyra would go back towards her old apartment and spy on the Krummers. If the car was not in the garage, there were chances she could meet them in Shopping Centre. It was very tactful of Riddy to stay indoors in such a situation when Skyra could take advantage of an opportunity. It kept Skyra tormented for 4 days. Skyra wanted the drama to unfold, and her perseverance was not in vain.

She saw them again. She had eye-contact with Riddy first; Bault was inside a shop, unaware. Riddy immediately underwent a change. She compressed herself to nothing- almost like a balloon excavating the air inside, within a blink's notice. Skyra looked at her bewildered, her guards down. Suddenly, she was aware of a strong force cutting through her aura. It was Bault. The whole transaction appeared to Skyra in an ultra-slow motion. Coming to senses after parting from them, she knew that she had survived it.

For the first time, Bault had taken such an aggressive initiative. And Skyra was stumped.

CHAPTER 31

FANTASY

Skyra had vowed to dethrone the Krummer supremacy. Thirteen of her army of 125 were already dead, but it had made a considerable headway. She felt like Joan of Arc, only she didn't want the ending she had.

The army, battling through the city, had now reached the premises of the Krummer Castle. Like a bolt of lightning, Skyra surged through the entrance of the castle. Her men clashed with the soldiers of the Krummer army. The Krummer army was more in number, but they appeared to be less competent than the opposing army.

Stepping inside the castle, she wrangled with the soldiers. Slowly, she went up the staircase. Now, not a soul blocked her way. The long-enduring wait was over. Her sword had reached the neck of the Countess.

"I was expecting a 'welcome back' from you, but I can suppose I heard that…", Skyra said to the Countess who was paralysed.

"So, let me have the privilege to ask, is your game over now…?? Or are you still pining to put me in your prison??", she paused, "Oh, the prison….!! I'm sorry for that…Please accept my condolences…"

Countess Ridaline didn't sputter a word.

"All this time, had you the intelligence to infer that you were messing with the wrong person?? The perfect victim you thought is actually the perfect anti-dote…"

Ridaline won't say anything. Skyra was clueless of the Krummer soldiers approaching behind her. Count Bault stood there, furious, watching the sword drop down from Skyra's hand.

"Capture her!!", Bault shouted to the soldiers.

CHAPTER 32

REALITY

The Krummers had taken the reins again on subconscious terms. But even though Skyra's self-esteem was damaged again and again, she was happy because now she was in action, and not huddled up in some corner. Moreover, this was a clean battle that she was fighting now. And she was fighting now, because she knew what her goal was- the Krummers had made it simple for her. And the goal would materialise only if she continued. There was no stopping for her now.

Even the universe had some laws governing its state, such as the planets that revolve in orbits. Even light has a limited speed. In the same way, there were laws that won't allow mental control to function beyond a limit. All she had to do was reach that point.

She was sick of the dreams she had been getting ever since the trouble with the Krummers had started brewing up. She wanted it to end, for once and for all. But that would happen only if the story was complete, and it had to have a happy ending. That was precisely what her goal was. The Count and the Countess had to be defeated by Queen Skyra. But the Queen had laid down her arms now. What would happen next?? To know that, Skyra had to see Ridaline.

Skyra hung around near the Krummer's apartment secretly, to observe the whereabouts of Riddy. After nearly a week of spying, she concluded that Riddy went out on Mondays, Wednesdays and Fridays by bus to her sculpting class at Krevon Street at 11:30 till 13:00.

Skyra appeared to be returning from somewhere after running an errand. As the two ladies crossed each other, Ridaline threw her glance sharply at Skyra. To Skyra, it felt like it had penetrated her skin. To speak the truth, she felt like a small schoolgirl in front of Ridaline's overwhelming presence.

CHAPTER 33

FANTASY

"Announce throughout the country the execution of the ousted queen after 3 days. The crowd of Helfung is invited to come with full enthusiasm…", Countess Ridaline commanded to the soldiers.

Chapter 34

REALITY

One more time. Just one more and I will be salvaged, Skyra said to herself. She mustered all her residual energy, arranged the shattered bits of her self-esteem and went to Shopping Centre. She wondered if Ridaline expected her. Expecting or not expecting, she wouldn't be venturing out without being prepared. That was enough justification.

This time, it was not just Ridaline who was the target, but even Bault had made his position important. Skyra, partly coldly and partly frantically, waited till the time had come. When she saw Bault, she did not find it necessary to look him in the eye. Her gaze was direct and indifferent. It said: "I have the immunity, I don't care". Watching him walk across, she thought she had just seen a man walk in a reverse evolutionary cycle.

When it was Ridaline's turn, Skyra's gaze seemed to say: "It's just a coincidence. No, I have not planned this." Then, her eyesight went deep into Ridaline's eyes till Riddy could not bear the shine and had to look down. She looked appalled beyond disbelief, like a scientist who had just discovered that his experiment had failed. As she trudged along, her steps got heavier; the vicious fumes inside her swelling her up. Skyra knew she didn't have to see her again.

CHAPTER 35

FANTASY

In the evening, the crowd had gathered around the colosseum. Skyra's hands were tied behind her back. The guillotine was kept in the centre. She closed her eyes.

When she opened them, she heard shouts of men. Henry had swung into the arena with a team of Prestorians, and fought savagely with the Krummer army, until they caught hold of the Count and Countess.

There was a brief pause in the pin-drop silence that followed. Suddenly, a voice from the crowd screamed, "Down with the Count!! Down with the Countess!!"

Then the whole crowd burst into shrieks. "Down with Helfung!!"

"We want Prestoria!!"

"Execute the Countess!!"

"Long live the Queen!!"

Skyra felt her hands being untied. She was released.

The Krummer Castle was converted into a prison with the renounced Count and Countess in it, by the orders of Skyra the reigning and functioning Queen. The land of Prestoria regained its existence, with the territory of Helfung amalgamated.

Chapter 36

REALITY

Skyra shifted to London. The dreams had stopped coming. At this point, she felt messed up. She had to straighten it all and streamline herself with people all over again. It was yet another new beginning for her. She had to establish her connection with the world again as a normal girl. But she knew her connection with Ridaline would stay lifelong.